THE
SECRET
BOX

THE SECRET BOX

WHITAKER RINGWALD

KATHERINE TEGEN BOOKS
An imprint of HarperCollins Publishers

Louisburg Library
Bringing People and Information Together

Katherine Tegen Books is an imprint of HarperCollins Publishers.

Library of Congress Cataloging-in-Publication Data
Ringwald, Whitaker.
The secret box / Whitaker Ringwald. — First edition.
pages   cm
Summary: "On her twelfth birthday, Jax Malone receives an odd,
unopenable present from an estranged aunt. When Jax and her
cousins Ethan and Tyler go on a quest to open the box, they uncover
a mystery with magical consequences"— Provided by publisher.
ISBN 978-0-06-221614-4 (hardcover bdg.)
[1. Secrets—Fiction.   2. Magic—Fiction.   3. Families—Fiction.]   I. Title.
PZ7.R4745Se 2014   2013008473
[Fic]—dc23   CIP   AC

Typography by Carla Weise
14 15 16 17 18   CG/RRDH   10 9 8 7 6 5 4 3 2 1
❖
First Edition

To Robert Gair, inventor of the box—
a most useful container for presents,
whatnots, and . . . *secrets.*

1

JAX

Saturday

It looked like an ordinary package.

Rectangular. Wrapped in brown paper. Sealed with strapping tape. Left on the doorstep with the rest of the mail. If Mom hadn't freaked out, I wouldn't have paid much attention to it. I would have thought it was just another boring present added to the most boring birthday ever. Why do birthdays lose their magic when you get older? I used to fight for a perfect corner of cake. Breaking the piñata seemed like candy raining from the sky. A balloon bouquet was awesome.

Popping it—even better.

"Give me that." Mom yanked the package from my hands. "You're not opening it."

"But it's got my name on it," I said, following her through the kitchen. The remaining half of my birthday cake sat on a platter, the fudge icing as thick as a quilt. Twelve red candles lay next to it, their wicks singed. I scurried through a pile of wrapping paper and past some gift boxes filled with the usual stuff—a pair of jeans, striped socks, lip gloss, nail polish, a couple of Starbucks cards. Big yawn. Hello? Didn't anyone hear me drop all those hints about a certain rhinestone-encrusted phone? My old phone had died and hadn't been replaced.

Years from now, if I looked back on this birthday, I wouldn't remember any of the other presents. But this new package had possibility. "Mom, why are you taking it away? It's for me."

"*She's* not supposed to send you anything."

"Who's not supposed to send me anything?"

Mom mumbled a name. It sounded like *Juniper* but I couldn't be sure. "Who?"

"Never mind," she snapped. She pushed open the kitchen's screen door and hurried toward her car, which was parked in the driveway. After opening the trunk, she tossed the package inside, then slammed the trunk shut. I stood in the doorway, watching as she relaxed her shoulders and took a long, deep breath, relief washing over her. Whatever the package contained, it was out of reach and out of sight. The way Mom was acting, she could have been guarding me from a rattlesnake, or a terrorist bomb.

"What are you going to do with it?" I asked.

She pushed her long brown hair behind her ears. Even though she always said I had beautiful hair, I'd spent my whole life wishing mine was like hers—silky and the color of caramel. My hair was so frizzy, trying to run a brush through it practically gave me a migraine. It was like yanking my brains out. "It's going back to where it came from."

Where had it come from? She'd grabbed the package before I'd had the chance to read the return address. This seemed totally unfair. "How come I don't get to open it?"

With quick, determined steps, Mom crossed the side yard and stood in front of me, her eyes narrowed, her finger pointing. "Listen to me, Jacqueline Alice Malone. You will not open that package. Do you hear me? If you open it, you'll be grounded for . . ." Her breath smelled like chocolate frosting. "For the rest of your life."

We'd stood face-to-face like this plenty of times, usually because I'd done something I wasn't supposed to do. And I'd been grounded plenty of times. But this time I hadn't done anything. *And* it was my birthday!

I could have argued with her. I'm pretty good at changing people's minds. But there was something different about the tone of her voice. She didn't sound mad. She sounded . . . *afraid*. "I don't understand why—"

"We're not going to talk about it," she interrupted. Then her expression softened and she hugged me. "I'm your mother and I only want what's best for you. Trust me." She squeezed harder. The hug felt desperate, as if she'd never see me again. Just when I started to get dizzy because I couldn't take a deep breath, her phone rang. She stepped away and fumbled through her pockets.

Trust her? This wasn't a matter of trust. Of course I trusted her. She was my mom, my only parent, the person who did everything for me. When I fell off my bike, who did I call? When my ex-best friend didn't invite me to her skating party, whose shoulder did I cry on? When I needed help with homework or help with life, she was the one I turned to.

But I can't stand secrets. A locked door, a sealed envelope, a whisper across the room—stuff like that drives me crazy. *No Trespassing. Off-limits. Keep Out.* Sometimes I think those signs are posted just to torture me. Call me curious or call me snoopy, I want to know what's going on.

And something was definitely going on. Because the only reason to keep me from opening that package was to hide whatever was inside.

What could it be? And who'd sent it?

I folded my arms and stared at the car trunk. Just a simple sheet of metal stood between me and a big fat secret. I imagined the package pulsing like a beating heart. An X drawn on it like a pirate map. A spotlight shining on the car's trunk.

"Hi, Mary," Mom said into her phone. Mary was her boss. "Hold on just a sec. I need to get a better signal." She pressed the phone to her chest and looked right into my eyes. "I'm taking that package to the post office when I get done with this call, so don't you dare stand there and make plans."

"*Moi?*" I smiled sweetly, trying to look innocent.

5

"You *know* what I mean."

"I'm not making plans," I lied. Of course I was making plans. Hello? I'm not a tortoise. If you stick me on a fence post I'm not going to sit there like a lump. I'm going to figure out a way to get where I want to go. And at that moment, I wanted to be inside that trunk.

One thing I know is this—if you want something badly enough, there's always a way.

Mom glared at me because she'd seen my sweet smile before. Then she walked back into the kitchen and slumped into a chair. "Okay, Mary, what's the problem now?" From her exasperated sigh, I could tell it was going to be a long conversation. Which meant I had some time before the package disappeared.

So while Mom ran her finger through frosting and listened to her boss, I raced upstairs to find the one person who would help me.

2
ETHAN

FACT: *Finland has over 187,000 lakes.*

I found that piece of information in a travel guide, a book I was reading when my cousin Jax burst into her bedroom.

"You'll never believe what just happened," she announced real loud.

I was stretched across a beanbag chair, my black Converse sneakers hanging off the ends of my toes. I'd gone upstairs to hide. There were ten people at Jax's birthday party. Ten is a group. I don't like groups because the conversation always feels like a jigsaw puzzle. No matter what I say, it never seems to fit. So I don't try much. Dad says I'm antisocial and if I always hide from people, I'll never have any friends. Mom, who has a degree in psychology, says I'm an introvert. My brother calls me a dweeb.

Why do we have to label everyone?

Jax slammed the door, then leaned against it as if someone had been chasing her. Her ponytail had come undone so her hair was hanging in her face. She was out of breath. She'd probably run up the stairs. She's always running everywhere, trying to get places faster than anyone else so she won't miss out on anything. My dad says Jax is gregarious. My mom says she's hyper. My brother says she's a pain.

She's my only friend. My best friend.

"I got a package and Mom won't let me open it. I think it came from someone named Juniper. I'm not sure."

I wasn't really paying attention. Jax tends to talk a lot. I held up *A Travel Guide to Finland*. Practically every book Jax owned was a travel guide. She collected them from garage sales. "Did you know that Donald Duck comics were banned in Finland because he doesn't wear pants?" I'd been reading the Fun Facts section. Facts help when you can't think of anything else to say.

"Will you please listen to me?" She yanked the book from my grip. "This is important."

Uh-oh. I recognized that pleading sound in her voice. Whenever Jax says *this is important*, it means she's going to try to talk me into doing something. I slowly sat up, staring at her through my bangs. Even though we're cousins we look totally different. Jax's skin is browner than mine, even during the summer. Her hair is jet black and she always wears it in a ponytail. My hair always looks like I've just taken my head out of the dryer.

I think she's pretty.

"My mom's going to return the package to the post office." Jax paced. "I want it back. I'm going to get it back."

I slid my feet into my sneakers and stood. "Uh . . . I think this is my cue to go home." I grabbed my baseball cap and plopped it on my head.

Jax darted around me, blocking the bedroom door with her skinny arms. There was no way I'd get past her. One year younger, but two inches taller, she'd proven time and time again that she could beat me in a wrestling match. It wasn't that she was stronger. It's just that I could never get a good grip on her because she squirmed so much.

9

"Wait," she begged. "We have to find out what's in that package."

"We?" I shoved my hands into my jeans pockets. "Why does it have to be *we*?" Jax always called us partners but I was more like the faithful sidekick. "Why can't it be *you* for once? Why do you always have to drag me into everything?"

"I don't drag you into everything. That's not fair." She lowered her arms. "Look, the thing is, it's my present. My name's on it. But my mom got really mad when she saw it and she said she was going to take it back to the post office. Then she mumbled the name Juniper."

"Who's Juniper?"

"Exactly! Who's Juniper?"

"Uh . . . I just asked that question."

"If we're both asking the same question, and we don't have the answer, then what we have is a mystery." She pushed aside some dirty clothes and slumped at the edge of her bed. "Why would someone I don't know send me a package? And why would my mom take it away? Do you think it has something to do with my dad?"

Silence fell over the room. Nobody knew who Jax's dad was, except of course Jax's mom. He'd disappeared

10

before Jax was born and other than Jax herself, he'd left no evidence of his existence—no photos, no old clothes, nothing. She used to imagine what he might look like or who he might be, which was always someone famous like a pop star, or an actor. But there was another possibility, as I'd stupidly pointed out one day. He could be a total loser. A drunk, a thief—maybe he was in jail. Just like me to say the wrong thing. She got real mad and we haven't talked about him since. I guess if you're going to create an imaginary dad, you might as well turn him into a prince.

If I could choose my dad, I'd pick the one I have. I'm lucky that way.

"If we follow my mom to the post office, we can get the package back. They put them into these bins. If you distract the people at the counter, then I can grab it."

"Uh . . . no way am I doing that. Tampering with the mail is a federal offense."

"I'm not tampering. My mother's the one who's tampering. It's my package. I'll just show my school ID and get it back." She leaned forward. "It was kinda heavy and rectangular. What do you think it is?"

I shrugged. "A book?"

"Jax?" Aunt Lindsay called from downstairs. She's Jax's mom. Jax's mom and my mom are sisters.

Jax sat up real straight. "Yeah?"

"They're short at the diner. I need to cover a shift for the rest of the afternoon. I'll be back around five thirty."

"Okay." She redid her ponytail. She was concocting a plan. I could practically see it streaming across her eyes like a headline across the bottom of a TV screen. *News Alert: Jax Malone is about to drag her cousin Ethan into another crazy scheme.* "We'll follow her. If she goes to the post office, we'll get the package and she'll never know. If she goes straight to the diner, we'll still get the package but after we see what's inside, we'll seal it up and put it back in the trunk so she'll never know."

"Uh . . . I'd like to remind you that you always say your mom will never know, but she always finds out. And we always get into trouble."

"Not this time. I promise."

How many times had I heard that? Jax makes "we won't get into trouble" promises as often as other people make their beds. "But—"

"Let's go." She started for the door, then stopped and smiled at me. "Don't worry. All the party guests are gone." She didn't think it was weird that I didn't like groups.

I followed her into the hallway. We stood on the top step, listening to the jingle of keys, then to footsteps, then to the thud of the kitchen door. "Come on." She hurried down the stairs.

I hesitated as a memory played in my mind. When we were little, we went to New York City to see a magician. During the show, Jax kept wondering how the magician's assistant had disappeared. I told her it was fake. There's no such thing as magic. But she wanted proof. So when our parents were in the lobby, Jax went behind the curtain to see if there was some kind of hole in the stage. There was. No big surprise. The big surprise was that I'd been dumb enough to follow her. *We won't get into trouble, I promise.* The stage manager caught us and there was a big scene. We got grounded for two weeks.

Aunt Lindsay's car engine started and wheels rolled over gravel as she backed out of the driveway. Jax reached into a terra-cotta planter that sat next to the front door. "Mom keeps an extra set of keys in here." She found it and shoved it into her pocket. Then she turned and stared up the stairs where I was still standing. "What are you waiting for?"

"Uh . . ." My fingers tapped the railing. I chewed my lower lip.

There is always a moment when my brain says, "This isn't going to end well." Why don't I ever listen? Is it because Jax's voice is louder than the one in my head?

"Ethan! Come on!"

Or maybe it's because without Jax, my life would be pretty boring. I mean, you can only read so many books. You can only spend so much time alone. So, pulling my baseball cap low, I hurried down the stairs and out the front door.

Because that's what a loyal sidekick does—he follows.

3
JAX

I pedaled so fast my thighs felt like they were on fire. Both the post office and the diner, where Mom worked, were on Main Street, which wasn't far. Why was Ethan so slow? He was the tortoise, I was the hare. Wait, back up. The hare loses the race, right?

"Come on!" I called.

The house we rented was on a shady street. All the houses around here were older. None of the driveways had fancy cars—not like in Ethan's neighborhood. There were no swimming pools, except for the kind you blow up. Most everyone had a dog, and they all barked as we rode past.

The sun was shining and a few extra cars were parked in front of the Smiths' house, thanks to a garage sale. Smith is such a boring name. Names are important. That's why I insist that my teachers and friends never call me Jacqueline. Jacqueline sounds prissy and proper, which isn't me. Jax has a nice ring to it, and there are no other kids named Jax at my school. Malone is an okay name, but it's Irish and doesn't quite fit me.

I wonder what my dad's last name is.

Normally I would have stopped to see what kind of stuff was for sale. I would have searched through the boxes of books. People always get rid of old travel guides. I guess if you're looking for a hotel or a fancy restaurant, you want the latest version. But I only cared about the photos. Cobble-stoned streets in medieval towns, chalets perched on snowcapped peaks, castles built on tiny islands that you can only walk to when the tide is low. Places far, far away from Chatham, New Jersey.

Don't get me wrong. Chatham is an okay place to live. We don't have bars on our windows and I can ride my bike most everywhere. The Passaic River winds past the town, and there's the usual stuff like a community swimming pool and some

16

nice parks. But I've been here my entire life—I've seen every square inch. Other than the Fishawack Festival, nothing much happens around here. We should have a Yawn Festival. Seriously. At least that would be something different.

It was too warm for my purple leather jacket, but I wore it anyway. I'd tucked the extra set of keys into one of its seven pockets. That jacket is my signature look. People might not know my name but at least they can say, "Oh, you mean the girl in the purple leather jacket? I've seen her."

We passed St. Patrick's Church. As I turned onto Lum Avenue, Ethan caught up with me. "I'm going to cut through the train station," I told him.

"I don't think that's a good idea. It's Saturday."

Why should it matter that it is Saturday? I wondered. But then the pop-up tents of the Saturday farmers' market came into view. Biking through the crowd would be tricky, but it was the quickest way to catch up with Mom. Luckily, it was one o'clock and the market had closed. The only people left were vendors tearing down their stands and loading their trucks. Ethan stayed close behind. He always complained about being dragged into my adventures, but I knew he secretly liked it. Without me, he'd just sit around and read. We were partners.

I darted around a fruit stand, then around a honey vendor's stand. Down the aisle I pumped, passing a woman who sold homemade jam, a family who raised llamas, and a couple of old ladies who knit baby hats. I barely missed a woman who was placing an order at a coffee cart. "Hi, Jax," she said with a wave. She was my English teacher, Ms. Buchanan.

"Hi," I called back. Mom didn't understand why I got a B minus in English. I tried to explain that Ms. Buchanan didn't teach the English I'm interested in. In her class we read a bunch of stuff written by a bunch of old men who died a million years ago. Shakespeare? Hello? Nobody talks like that anymore. And then we read Homer. He wrote all this stuff about Greek gods. I almost had a stroke, it was so boring. Who cares?

"Watch out!" a man yelled as I narrowly missed a crate that held a live rooster. The rooster squawked and rustled its red feathers.

"Sorry!"

A few more swerves and I reached Main Street. After skidding to a stop, I turned around to search for Ethan. He'd decided to walk his bike between the vendors, his head down so he didn't have to make eye contact. He looked so serious, as if he was going to see the doctor about a brain tumor. I sighed. Seemed like I was always waiting for him to catch up. "You almost killed that rooster," he said when he reached me.

"Wasn't even close." I kept my balance with one foot. "So, do you see my mom?"

Ethan leaned on his handlebars, his gaze scanning the street. Then he pointed. Mom hadn't turned right to the post office. She'd turned left and was pulling into the diner's parking lot. That meant the package was still safe inside the trunk.

We locked our bikes in a rack outside the hardware store. Then we crossed the street and stood in the alley between the diner and the shoe store. "Uh . . . I'm guessing you have a plan?" Ethan said.

"A plan? *Moi?*"

He groaned.

"Just teasing. Of course I have a plan. You stand guard while I open the trunk." When I needed someone to stand guard, Ethan was my go-to guy.

"Yeah, okay," he mumbled, pulling a paperback book out of his back pocket.

"Oh no you don't," I said. Ethan couldn't stand

guard and read at the same time. I'd learned this when I'd tried to sneak a bag of garbage into Mr. Smith's can because ours was totally full. Ethan was supposed to be standing guard but he'd been reading. Shoving trash into someone else's can is against neighborhood rules. Mr. Smith caught me in the act. Grounded. One week.

"Yeah, okay." Ethan tucked the book back into his pocket.

Why did he always look so serious? This was fun!

It was easy to see inside the Chatham Diner, thanks to the big picture windows out front. Most of the tables were full. The diner was the best place in town for breakfast, which they served all day and night. The pancakes with crumbled bacon inside the batter are my personal favorite. Mom, already in her apron and name tag, was filling glasses with ice water. Ethan started tiptoeing up to the entry. "Why are you tiptoeing?" I asked. "Tiptoeing looks suspicious."

He frowned at me. Spying didn't come naturally to him. Then he crouched behind a newspaper kiosk. "Okay," he called, peering around its edge. "I can see her. She's busy."

"Whatever you do, don't take your eyes off her."
Then, after a deep breath, I walked *calmly* across
the parking lot toward Mom's car. Even though my
heart pounded and my palms had turned sweaty,
I took slow, steady steps. If you act like you're up
to something, then everyone will know you're up
to something. I wouldn't have been caught on that
magician's stage if Ethan hadn't been wringing his
hands and looking totally guilty. Sometimes I have
to remind myself that we're cousins, since we're so
different.

With the key pinched between my fingers,
I took a quick look around. Ethan gave me a
thumbs-up so I slid the key into the lock. *Click.*
The trunk popped open. My fingers felt electrified
as I reached inside. I wanted that package more
than I'd wanted anything in a long time. I kinda
expected it to jump into my arms, like a puppy. We
were meant to be together.

My plan was this—I'd carefully peel back the
tape and unwrap the brown paper. If I found a card
tucked inside, I'd keep it. Mom would never know.
But the present itself would have to be resealed. If
it turned out to be something boring, like a book
I'd already read or another pair of socks, then I

wouldn't care when she returned it to the post office. But if it was something amazing . . .

My fingers reached all around. Where was it? I leaned inside the trunk. A pair of running shoes, some canvas tote bags, an old first-aid kit, but nothing else. Where—?

"Hi, Jax."

"Ouch." My head bumped on the trunk's lid. "Hi. Jeez, you almost gave me a heart attack."

"Sorry. Didn't mean to sneak up on you." Michael stood next to the car, his white T-shirt stained with grease, his hair covered by a blue bandana. He worked in the diner's kitchen during the summers when he was back from college. He was my favorite cook because he could scramble an egg so it was fluffy, not gooey. "What's going on?" he asked. As he yawned, he shifted a package to his other arm.

My package! Cue the choir.

"Nothing's going on," I said, managing a casual smile. I glanced over at Ethan, who was totally distracted because he was reading the newspaper through the kiosk glass. He hadn't even noticed Michael and the package walk right past him. Yeesh. After closing the trunk, I slipped the key into my pocket. "What's going on with you?"

"I'm heading home to bed. These morning shifts are killing me. I don't know why we have to open at five A.M. It should be against the law to eat breakfast that early." He yawned again.

"Whatcha got there?" I asked, pointing to the package. The words *Return to Sender* had been written across the front in red ink.

"Your mom wanted me to take this to the post office. See ya later." Moving like a sloth, he headed for the sidewalk.

"Hey, Michael," I said, following. The scent of bacon floated around him like a cloud. "I could deliver that for you. I'm going that way."

Michael pressed the crosswalk button. His next yawn stretched every muscle in his face as if his skin was made of Play-Doh. "Yeah? You don't mind?"

I clenched my teeth, keeping myself from breaking into a crazy grin. "Mind? No, I don't mind. No problem." I reached out eagerly, my fingers twitching. *Give. Me. The. Package.*

"Your mom kinda made me promise to do it myself." He rubbed the back of his neck. "Maybe I should—"

"I won't tell her," I said. "She'll never know. You go get some sleep."

"Sounds good to me." He set the package in my hands. "I won't tell if you won't tell."

When the brown paper touched my skin, I shivered as if I'd just been given a passport and a plane ticket to Paris. "See ya," I said as Michael wobbled away, drunk on exhaustion. I couldn't have planned it better. I didn't have to tamper with the mail. I didn't have to reseal the package. And I didn't have to convince Ethan to stand guard outside the post office, which would have been tricky. I could keep it. It was the best of all possibilities.

Ethan was still hunched in front of the kiosk. How could I be mad at him? He liked to read. Seriously, a marching band could have strolled past and he wouldn't have noticed. I tapped him on the shoulder.

"Ahhh," he blurted, nearly jumping out of his skin.

"Whatcha reading?"

"An article about global warming," he said. Then he glanced at the package. "So, are we done?"

"Almost."

We didn't say another word until we'd reached

our bikes and the package was safely concealed in my bike basket, under my purple jacket. Now to find a place safe from prying eyes. "To the park," I said.

We rode to Memorial Park and found an empty bench. A few people were walking their dogs and some kids were heading into the pool, but I didn't recognize anyone. Ethan sat next to me, his shoulder pressed against mine. I ran a finger over the return address. "Juniper Vandegrift," I read. "Never heard of her."

"Me neither."

"She lives in New Hope, Pennsylvania," I said, tracing the city and zip code.

I turned the package over. Was this the first birthday present Juniper had sent, or had Mom been returning them my whole life? Why would she do that? What was she protecting me from?

I began to peel back the strapping tape. A shiver made the hairs on the back of my neck stand up. The box wouldn't contain a pair of jeans, or striped socks, or a Starbucks card.

Somehow I knew that whatever lay inside would be anything but boring.

4
ETHAN

FACT: *Strapping tape is stronger than masking tape because it has these filaments that are made from fiberglass. Masking tape was invented back in the 1930s to help auto painters paint clean lines.*

Most people think those kinds of facts are boring. My brain is loaded with them.

I sat next to Jax on the bench. Using her fingernails, she loosened one edge of the tape. She'd gotten the package without us having to break any laws, and it looked like we might not get grounded this time. But why was she peeling so slowly? She never did anything slowly.

"Want to use my knife?" I asked, pulling my Swiss army knife from my pocket.

"No thanks." She tossed the first piece of strapping tape aside. Then she paused, her fingers lingering over the next piece. I think she was savoring the moment. I always did the same thing before scratching a Christmas lottery ticket. Until the truth was revealed, anything was possible.

I wiped my forehead with my sleeve. The bench was shaded by an elm tree but I'd worked up a sweat during the bike ride. Even though summer had just begun, it was already hot. According to that article I'd read about global warming, our local meteorologist predicted temperatures higher than normal. Weather patterns were changing all over the world. "Did you know the last two decades were the hottest in four hundred years?"

"Hmmm," Jax said, still picking with her fingernail.

Sunlight glinted off the army knife. It was called the Swiss Champ, one of the most popular because it had almost everything—a can opener, a wood saw, a

27

magnifying lens; it even had a fish scaler. My name was engraved on it. "You sure you don't want to use this?"

Jax ran out of patience with the tape and ripped the paper. "Ouch," she said, holding out her finger. A perfect red line formed across the tip. "I hate paper cuts." She winced and turned away as the first drops of blood oozed out. "Ethan . . ." she pleaded.

Jax could never be a doctor. She hates blood. The worst time was when we'd been riding our bikes home from school a couple of years ago and she fell off and gashed her knee on a rock. The blood drenched her pants and she got so grossed out, she vomited. I helped by wrapping my T-shirt around her knee. Blood didn't bother me. I'd been cursed with nosebleeds most of my life so I was used to it.

It's strange because Jax can do just about anything without worrying or getting freaked out. It doesn't make much sense that blood would be a problem. No one else in the family is like that. Mom says it's a phobia.

I grabbed some repair tape from my bike kit and wound it around her finger. "Thanks," she said, color returning to her face.

"No problem." I sat back on the bench.

"How 'bout a drum roll?" She jabbed me with her

elbow. "Come on, do a drum roll."

I glanced around to make sure no one was watching. Then I rolled my tongue and tried but a bunch of spit flew out. Jax giggled. "That sounds more like a fart. You do it like this . . ." She rolled her tongue and smacked her palms against the bench. Her drum roll was so loud, a few people turned and looked. Then she tore the rest of the paper and tossed it aside.

A metal box lay on Jax's lap, about the size of a small jewelry box with a little screen set into the top. "Looks like an LED screen," I said.

"Do you see a card or a note?"

I searched around our feet and under the bench in case something had fallen out. "Nothing. Maybe it's inside."

Jax tried to open the box but there was no obvious opening and no hinges. "You try," she said, handing it to me.

I ran my fingers along the box and found a seam, perceptible only by touch. Then I found something else. "It's a button," I said, pressing it.

We both gasped as the screen lit up.

Jax and I leaned close. A message appeared.

Attempt 1 of 10.

Those words disappeared and another message appeared.

190 miles from the right spot.

Jax looked at me, her eyebrows raised. "There's a right spot? What does that mean?" Then that message disappeared and the word *Good-bye* took its place. The screen went black.

Jax grabbed the box and pushed the button. The screen lit up with a slightly different message.

Attempt 2 of 10.
190 miles from the right spot.
Good-bye.

"Weird," she whispered. She pushed again.

Attempt 3 of 10.

"Uh . . . maybe you shouldn't keep pushing it," I said. She always does that, pushes buttons over and over as if it will make a difference. Like in the elevator. Or at a vending machine. It drives me crazy. The potato-chip bag will not drop any faster.

She pushed again.

Attempt 4 of 10.

"I don't get it," she complained.
"Wait!"

Attempt five of ten.
190 miles from the right spot.
Good-bye.

I covered the button with my hand. "It said attempt *five* of ten. That means we only have five attempts left."

"Five attempts to do what?"

"Uh . . ." I shrugged. "To open it?"

"Oh. That makes sense." Her cheeks were a bit red and sweat dotted her nose. "I wonder what's inside." She shook the box gently. Nothing rattled or moved. "Maybe we can pry it open with your knife."

I tried to stick the blade into the seam but it wouldn't fit.

"Does your dad have an axe?" she asked.

"I don't think so." I'd never seen my dad chop wood. Our fireplace was gas. I put the knife back into my pocket. "I think you'll have to solve the puzzle if you want to get it open."

Jax smiled. "I'm pretty good at puzzles." She set the box back on her lap. "Okay, let's figure this out. It said we're not in the right spot. That means the box has to be in a certain place before it will open. But how can a box know where it is?"

"It must have a GPS unit." Fact: GPS stands for global positioning system.

"So then, how do we find the right spot?"

We sat in silence for a few moments, staring at the strange birthday present. A woman and her German shepherd walked past. A jogger stopped to tie his shoe. I tried to come up with an answer. "We could go to different places and press the button," I said. "But that seems random. And the GPS reading only gives us distance, it doesn't give us direction. I bet there's some sort of formula we could use."

"Formula?" she asked. "You mean math?"

"Yeah, math." I frowned because neither Jax nor I liked math.

"Forget math. I'm going to get an axe."

Jax threw the paper and tape into a garbage can. But she saved the upper left-hand corner, where Juniper Vandegrift's return address was written. She folded it carefully and tucked it into her pocket. Then she set the metal box into her bike basket, concealing it with her purple jacket.

We rode back to her house. As soon as we got there, we dumped the bikes on the lawn, then stood in front of Mr. Smith's house. The garage sale was in full swing. "He's got an axe in his woodpile," Jax said. "On the side of the house."

"I don't think hacking at the box is a good idea," I pointed out. "What if you break whatever's inside?"

"I won't break anything," she said. "I'll just whack the corner off, just enough to at least get a peek." She stood real close and lowered her voice. "Okay, so you go over there and ask Mr. Smith a bunch of questions to distract him while I get the axe."

"Uh . . . why don't you just ask him if you can borrow it?"

"Hello? He hates me, remember? He caught me cutting roses off his bush and didn't care that they were for Mom." She gave me a little shove. "Go distract him. This is important."

I hate doing stuff like this. I'd be perfectly happy to never cause a distraction.

Pulling my baseball cap real low, I walked into Mr. Smith's yard. What would I say? Would I pretend to be looking for something, like old vinyl records or comic books? Stuff was strewn all over the grass—wooden chairs, a rocking horse, a croquet set. A card table wobbled beneath the weight of vases, books, and mismatched plates. Mr. Smith was talking to a man about a rusty lawnmower. Sounded like they were bickering over price.

Crash.

I whipped around. The card table had toppled over. A toddler was standing next to it. He scrunched up his face and began to wail. His mom picked him up as Mr. Smith hurried over to see what had happened. The distraction had nothing to do with me. Jax raced around the house, then reappeared with the axe in her hand. I suppose that running with an axe is just as dangerous as running with scissors, but she didn't seem to care. She grabbed the box from her bike basket, then raced into her garage.

As Mr. Smith tried to bully the mom into paying for the broken vases, I made my escape. I expected to find the box all mangled, but when I got inside the garage, Jax was holding the box. The axe lay on the floor. "I couldn't do it," she said, her face flushed. "I had this strange feeling. I couldn't hurt it."

"Hurt it?" That seemed like a weird thing to say.

"You mean *dent* it?"

"What if I ruined whatever's inside?" She ran her hand over the box. "What did you say about a formula?"

"I said that I bet there's some sort of math formula that will help us solve the puzzle."

She peered out the garage door. "We need to find someone who can help."

We both took a deep breath and said, at the same time, "Tyler." Then we cringed. Because in a perfect world, we'd never have to see or talk to Tyler. My older brother.

5

ETHAN

FACT: *Scientists have confirmed that some people are born good at math. It has to do with this thing called number sense. I don't have it. Neither does Jax. But my brother, Tyler, has about as much of it as a person can have.*

Jax and I equally disliked Tyler and it wasn't just because he was obnoxious. There was the whole rude thing, and the ego-bigger-than-his-head thing. But Jax only had to deal with Tyler on a part-time basis. I lived with the guy. It wasn't easy growing up in the shadow of a genius who constantly reminded you that he was a genius. "Hey, noob, don't trip on my Mathlete trophy." "Hey, idjot, hand me my Science Olympian trophy so I can polish it." "Hey, brainsap, better protect your eyes from the awesome gleam of my chess trophy." Our dad had shelves built in the office just to hold Tyler's trophies.

I won a trophy once, for T-ball. We'd lost every game but the parents gave each of us a trophy because we'd "tried hard" and they didn't want us to feel bad about ourselves. Just once, I'd like to win a trophy that wasn't given to me out of pity—a trophy I'd actually earned. I know it sounds pathetic, but if it could be bigger than any of Tyler's trophies, that would be great.

We biked to my house, which was about a mile from Jax's. My parents had the house built with us kids in mind, so there was a family room with a pool table, a shed for our bikes, and a tennis court in the side yard. It was my job to mow the lawn, but a gardener took care of the other stuff. I have no idea how to prune roses.

My parents were at work. They own a toy-testing company in town. Tyler was up in his room. No surprise. "What?" he barked as I knocked. A sign taped to his door read, *Embrace the Zombie Apocalypse*.

If this summer was anything like last summer,

he'd spend most of it perched in front of his computer, his skin growing paler by the day. I opened the door and we stepped into his cave. Jax held the box in her arms, concealing it with her coat.

The curtains were drawn so the screen provided the only light, casting its glow on Tyler's hunched shoulders. The voices streaming from the speakers belonged to his gaming friends, who were also locked away in their rooms. "Shove off," Tyler grumbled.

Jax scrunched her nose. It always smelled bad in there, like sweat and something rotten. Bags of chips littered the carpet, along with soda and energy-drink cans. For someone so smart, Tyler sure was a slob. The only things he cleaned were the trophies.

"Uh . . ." I hesitated, because I hated what I was about to say. "We need your help."

"I'm busy. Invasion in progress." His fingers flew across his gaming mouse and keyboard, his legs twitching as if he were running a marathon. "Gotcha!" A Cyclops's head smashed into a pillar.

"Way to go!" a nasal voice said from somewhere in cyberspace.

"Check your health bar. Did you take damage?"

"Negative. Choosing new weapon. Power axe enabled."

Another Cyclops lumbered down a dark tunnel. Tyler took aim with a glowing sword and WHAM! the head flew across the screen. Tyler snickered, then chugged some soda.

The game was called Cyclopsville and Tyler and his buddies had been developing it all year. It had started as a school project but had become an obsession. Tyler created the story and wrote the dialogue. He loved mythology, so he crammed it with all sorts of Greek and Roman monsters. His friend Walker designed the graphics. The other two friends were developing the game engine.

WHAM! Another Cyclops's head was severed. "There's not enough blood," Tyler said into his mic. "The blood should coat the ground and walls, maybe some guts could hang from the ceiling. Can you do that?"

"Sure," Walker's voice replied.

Jax and I had agreed on the bike ride over that we wouldn't tell Tyler the truth about where we got the metal box. Neither of us trusted him. And I had nothing to use for blackmail so if he wanted to turn me in, I wouldn't be able to stop him.

"Tyler," Jax said. "We're serious. We need your help."

"I have zero interest in your petty problems."

I sighed. It was useless. Tyler was lost in his world. He could play all day and all night if my parents let him, and often they did. Only a natural disaster could have forced him from his game. Or a boost to his ego . . .

No way. I was *not* going to flatter my brother. But Jax, as if reading my mind, was ready and willing.

"Please help us," she pleaded. Then she looked at me and rolled her eyes. "Because . . . because we're not smart enough to help ourselves. You're so much smarter than us."

Tyler's fingers froze. He sat up straight. "Hey, guys," he told his friends. "I need to pause the game for a minute. Prioritization code, Family Interference." He muted the microphone, then spun around in his chair and pushed his dark hair off his forehead. His T-shirt had sweat stains under the pits and the pi symbol on the front. He stared at us with a dazed expression as his focus turned from the mythic landscape of Cyclopsville to his dark, humid room. "It's about time you two acknowledged your intellectual inferiority."

Now it was my turn to roll my eyes.

After setting her coat aside, Jax held out the box.

Its metallic surface reflected Tyler's computer screen. "What's that?" he asked.

"I got it at a garage sale," she explained. "It won't open. But if you push this button, the screen lights up with a message. It's a puzzle."

"A puzzle?" One of Tyler's eyebrows arched. He was intrigued. His hand darted out and, before Jax could react, he pushed the button.

Attempt 6 of 10.
193 miles from the right spot.
Good-bye.

"Jeez Tyler, you just wasted a push," Jax grumbled as she stepped away. "Don't do that again. Now we only have four pushes left."

"It's got a GPS unit," I said. "We have to go to a preprogrammed place in order for it to open."

Tyler curled his upper lip. "Duh. That's obvious."

Jax shuffled in place, her arms wrapped around the box. "So how would you find the right spot if your only clue is that it's one hundred and ninety-three miles away?"

Tyler snorted. "You're interrupting my game for something as easy as that? What a couple of

41

morooons." He spun back around and reached for the gaming mouse.

"I'm not a morooon, whatever that is," Jax snapped. "And neither is Ethan. Why are you always so mean? Why can't you just help us?"

"What's in it for me?" Tyler asked, his back to us. "Are you going to give me whatever's in the box?"

"No way," Jax said, her grip tightening.

"Then why should I help you?"

I wasn't one bit surprised. We should have known better than to ask my brother for help. Being smart didn't have anything to do with being kind or generous. "Let's go," I said, heading for the door.

"No, wait. I want to figure this out." Jax's gaze darted around the room. "Oh, I know. I got two Starbucks cards for my birthday. You can have them."

"Caffeine as payment?" Tyler spun around. "Deal." He held out his palm, fingers wiggling. Jax tucked the box under her arm, reached into her back pocket, and pulled out a thin purple wallet. Then she handed over the Starbucks cards. "Payment accepted," Tyler said. After grabbing an atlas off his shelf, he pushed aside a bunch of candy-bar wrappers to make room on his desk. "Gather round, minions, and I shall educate your feeble minds."

Jax set the metal box on the bed and we both leaned over Tyler's shoulders, watching as he searched through the atlas's index until he found a map of the eastern coast of the United States. He rifled through his drawer for a pen, then drew a dot on the map, right over Chatham. "The key to solving your riddle is geometry. This dot is approximately where I pushed the button." He grabbed a ruler and took a measurement from the atlas's key. He drew a line out from the dot and into the ocean. "And this is one hundred and ninety-three miles away, the distance to the right spot."

"It's in the water?" I asked.

"Maybe," he said. Then, using a compass, he drew a circle around the Chatham dot with a radius of 193. "Somewhere on this circle you'll find what you're looking for." He grabbed his can of soda and took a long drink. "Lesson concluded. Now go play with your little box." He reached for his mouse again.

Jax grabbed the atlas. "But this circle goes through Massachusetts, Vermont, New York, Pennsylvania . . . it goes through six states. We only have four more times to push the button. We can't go to all those places."

"Is there a way to narrow the search?" I asked.

Tyler grimaced, as if I'd asked him to give me one of his kidneys. "Jeez. Didn't either of you take geometry? You'll need another reading, *obviously.*"

"Where?" Jax asked.

"Somewhere outside of Chatham. Push the button again and you'll find out how far you are from the right spot." He tapped his fingers on the desk, eager to get back to his game. "Then you'll draw another circle. Get it?"

We both shook our heads.

"What do you mean you don't get it? I went to the same middle school that you guys go to. Have they fired all the math teachers?"

We shook our heads again.

"Unbelievable. This is the state of our public education system." He drew two circles on a piece of paper. "The circles will overlap in two places. One of those two places will be the right spot." Then, with a sneer he added, "Duh." He spun around in his chair, unmuted his microphone, and said, "Gentlemen, I have returned. Commence Operation Cycloptocide."

"Reload from previous checkpoint."

"Welcome back, Commander."

Even though he was a complete jerk, Tyler had a whole mess of friends. Even though I was a nice guy,

I didn't. Sometimes it works out that way.

Jax picked up the piece of paper. She stared at the two circles for a moment, her face clenched with confusion. "How far should we—?"

"No more questions, dweebs. Be gone." Tyler acted like a king dismissing his servants, only this king had pimples and had never been on a date.

"Come on," I said. I didn't totally understand the math but I knew we'd figure it out.

But Jax stood her ground. "I have one more question, Tyler, and I'm not going anywhere until you answer it. And you know I'm totally capable of standing here all day, in your room, bugging you."

He groaned. "Fine. One more question."

"You ever heard of Juniper Vandegrift?"

"She's our great-aunt." He pressed the mouse and his body jerked. "Whoa! Did you see that? I got him right in his one eye."

"We have a great-aunt?" I asked.

"Yeah. She's Mom's and Lindsay's aunt, so that makes her our *great*-aunt."

Jax leaned against the desk. "How come you know about her and we don't?"

"'Cause you two were babies when she had the big fight with Aunt Lindsay." He scooted to the edge of his chair. "Hey, Walker, that dangling eyeball is a great effect."

"Thanks," Walker's voice said.

"What was the fight about?" Jax asked.

"I don't know. But she must have done something bad because our parents said she was never welcome in our family again. Now get lost. You're interrupting the campaign. Watch out, Skywalker! Forces of chaos invading." The screen filled with splashing blood.

Just before I closed the door, Tyler added, "Farewell, inferior life forms."

"My brother is such a sweet guy," I said as we left his cave behind.

I expected Jax to add another sarcastic comment, because one of the things that fueled our friendship was our mutual contempt for my brother. But instead, she smiled. "This is the most amazing thing that's ever happened to me." Excitement danced in her brown eyes. "We have a great-aunt we didn't even know about and my mom is trying to keep me from opening her present." She wrapped her purple coat around the metal box and hurried down the hall. "Come on. Let's go catch the next train."

"Train?"

"Yeah." Jax led the way through my house. She

stopped to grab an orange from the fruit bowl. "We need to get outside Chatham for a second reading and we can't get far enough on our bikes. We'll be back before my mom gets off her shift and before your parents get home from work. You won't get into trouble, I promise."

Where had I heard that before?

6
JAX

It turned out my family had a whole bunch of secrets that were as juicy as grapes.

There was the secret about my father, a man my mom always refused to talk about. He did the biological bit—helped create me—then disappeared, never to be seen again. No matter how much I pleaded, no matter how much I snooped, I never learned anything more about him. I knew that Mom and Aunt Cathy were keeping something from me because there were lots of times when I'd walk into a room and their conversation would stop.

So I tried to spy. Whenever my mom and my

aunt were in a huddle, I'd stick in my earbuds and pretend to be listening to music, but the eavesdropping never worked. The cup-to-the-wall thing didn't work either. And each time I lay on the floor and tried to listen under the door, I ended up inhaling dust balls and my coughing gave me away.

But now there was a new secret—a great-aunt. Juniper Vandegrift. What a cool name. It sounded important. According to the return address, she didn't live very far away. But why had she and Mom gotten into a fight? Clearly it was a big deal, otherwise she'd visit us during the holidays. We'd talk on the phone. We'd do all the normal things people do with their great-aunts. Like open birthday presents.

As usual, I didn't have much money in my wallet, but Ethan did and he offered to buy my train ticket. I hate feeling like a charity case, so while he stood at the ticket machine, I thought about jumping the turnstile. The transit police were nowhere to be seen. I could probably get away with it.

"Here," he said, handing me a round-trip ticket.

"Thanks. I'll pay you back."

What would I do without Ethan? I gave him a hug. He turned red and tugged on his baseball cap.

We settled into some seats, the box tucked safely into my backpack, which I kept on my lap so no one could steal it. "Is it hot in here?" I asked.

"No." He pointed to a vent. "The air conditioner is on."

I wrapped my arms around the backpack. "Sure feels hot to me."

An hour later, we got off at Penn Station in New York City. This has to be one of the most exciting places in the world! Every kind of sound, every kind of smell, every kind of person, every kind of food—all underground. Hoagies, gyros, iced coffee. Turbans, dreadlocks, braids. Brakes screeching, heels pounding, perfume mixing with B.O. Everyone going somewhere fast. A gigantic board showed all the destinations to choose from.

"Ethan, isn't this place great?" Where was he? Clutching the backpack, I spun around. "Ethan?"

He stood next to a vending machine, his back pressed against the station wall, his eyes wide. Poor guy. He hated crowds. "Are you okay?"

"It's too loud." He looked like he might get sick.

"We won't stay long," I assured him. "Do you think the GPS unit will work down here?"

"We should probably go up to street level."

He followed me up the escalator. The city greeted us with honking horns, bright sunlight, and tons of tourists wearing *I Love NYC* T-shirts and posing for photos. We found a spot under an awning. I opened the backpack, pulled out the box, and pressed the button. Huddled together, Ethan and I watched as the screen lit up.

```
Attempt 7 of 10.
206 miles from the right spot.
Good-bye.
```

"Uh . . . can we go now?" Ethan asked, chewing on his lower lip.

"Sure."

We were pretty quiet on the train ride back. Ethan read some tourist brochures. No doubt he'd be sharing some facts with me. Kids teased him when he did that at school. They didn't understand it was his way of trying to be friendly.

I stared at the commuters, wondering if any could be my great-aunt Juniper. Did she have black frizzy hair like me or shaggy brown hair like Ethan? Was she shy or outgoing? Did she like purple? I wrapped my arms tightly around the backpack. Why was Mom mad at her?

As soon as we got to my house, we hurried up to my room. It was almost dinnertime but Mom wasn't home yet. Ethan texted Aunt Cathy to tell her that he'd be home in an hour. After setting the box on my bed, I found a compass and ruler in the back of my desk drawer. Then I tried to remember Tyler's instructions. Make a circle . . . draw a line . . . something about geometry.

I hadn't paid much attention in geometry. News alert: measuring angles and lines is about as exciting as clipping your toenails. Those minutes in class had ticked so slowly, I started to think that somebody had poured molasses into the clock.

"What are we supposed to do again?" I asked Ethan.

He downloaded a map of the eastern coast of the United States, printed it, then set it on my desk. "The first readings were roughly one ninety." Slowly and precisely, he drew a line just like Tyler had drawn, then using the compass he created a circle. I leaned over his shoulder. "You're breathing in my ear."

"Sorry," I said.

He rearranged the ruler. "The reading we did

in New York was two hundred and six." Ever so slooooowly, he drew another line. I tapped my feet. *You're not getting graded on this, so hurry it up,* I almost said. He drew another circle. We both leaned over the map. The circles intersected in two places.

I pointed to one of the intersections, which lay in the middle of Lake Oneida in New York State. "We'll need a boat if we want to go there. I don't know how we'd do that." I pointed to the second intersection. "Hey, that's Washington, DC. That's easy to get to. Let's try that first."

"You want to go to DC?" Ethan asked.

"I want to open the box. DC makes a lot more sense than a lake. Besides, Juniper wouldn't send me out on the water. That would be totally dangerous."

Ethan chewed on the end of the pencil. "Do you think your mom will let you take the train to DC?"

I sat on the edge of my bed and released a long sigh, like a leaking balloon. No way would Mom let me go to Washington, DC, on my own. She was as protective as a momma bear. I think being a single parent made her feel that she had to be both my dad and my mom, so she went a little crazy sometimes trying to fill both roles. And I'd gotten into some trouble lately, so she didn't totally trust me anymore. She was still mad at me for the whole grocery-store incident.

Let's get one thing straight—I'm not a shoplifter. I was just wondering how it would feel. I was standing in the candy section and I thought about how easy it would be to stick a Snickers bar up my sleeve. If I acted normal, no one would know. I could walk right out the door. So I did. But as soon as I got outside, I felt really bad and I turned around to put it back.

I wasn't fast enough.

Turns out they have security cameras all over the place and someone had been watching me. The manager called Mom and I thought she was going to explode when she stormed into the office at the back of the store. "Jacqueline Alice Malone," she hissed, her face bright red. "What were you thinking?" She was wearing her apron and name tag from the diner.

I didn't know how to explain it. "I'm sorry."

The manager agreed not to call the police as long as I didn't come into his store again without adult supervision. I felt like a baby who needed a sitter.

"Why?" Mom asked when we got into the car. "Why would you steal?"

"I just wanted to try," I said with a shrug. "I was going to put it back."

"You wanted to try?" She gripped the steering wheel until her fingers turned white. "Have you done this before?" I shook my head. She took a long breath, released her hands, and looked into my eyes. "Listen to me very carefully. Stealing is wrong. And it's not the life I want for you."

"Life? What are you talking about?" Jeez, was she overreacting or what? "It was just a candy bar. It's not like I'm trying to be a career criminal."

"Career criminal?" She clenched her jaw. "Don't do it again. Ever. Do you promise?"

"Yeah, okay. I won't do it again."

I hadn't told Ethan. It was way too embarrassing. I'd shared most everything with him but not *that*.

So how could I get to Washington, DC? If the candy-bar incident had happened a few months ago, maybe Mom would have cooled off by now. But it had happened just last week, so the memory was still fresh. "We're going to have to get someone to take us," I told Ethan.

"Us?" He groaned. "When did I volunteer?"

He hadn't, of course, but we were partners. "We'll need a chaperone."

"Who?"

"Tyler," I said.

Ethan cringed. "No way. I'm not driving all the way to Washington, DC, with my brother."

"Why not? He's got a driver's license *and* a car."

"Why not?" Ethan's voice cracked. It had started doing that lately. "Uh . . . well, the first reason is because he's a terrible driver. It took him four tries to get his license. He couldn't figure out how to parallel park so he blamed it on the car."

"Then we won't let him parallel park," I said.

"Okay, but the second reason is he'll make us listen to his gaming music."

"We'll wear headphones. That'll work."

"Maybe." Ethan rearranged himself in the desk chair. "But there are other reasons, like—"

"I know all the reasons," I interrupted, summoning my confident voice, the one I used when I needed to convince Ethan to help me. "I know Tyler's a pain. But we can't ask your parents to take us, and we can't ask my mom to take us. We have to keep the box a secret. Tyler's the only choice." I grabbed the box off the bed and held it in front of Ethan. His face was reflected in its gleaming surface. "This is really, really, really important to me. I need your help. Please?"

Ethan crossed his arms and grumbled under his breath. "Yeah, okay."

"Yay!" I cheered, happy that I was going to solve this mystery but also happy that Ethan was going to be there with me—because going on this adventure without him would be like going to Disneyland alone. And who wants to ride Space Mountain solo?

"Now we have to figure out how to convince Tyler." I glanced at the alarm clock next to my bed. It was getting close to dinnertime. Mom would be home soon. "He's already seen the box and he knows we're trying to solve the puzzle. Do you think I should tell him the truth? It would make things a lot easier."

"Sure, you can tell him the truth," Ethan said. "If you want him to blackmail you for the *rest of your life*. Remember when he found out I got a D on my history test? I'd stuffed the test in the bathroom garbage can and he found it and basically made my life a living hell. I had to dust all his Star

Wars figurines and wash all his socks by hand. *By hand.* Have you smelled Tyler's socks?"

"Yeah, I remember." The blackmail wasn't a surprise. Tyler often used blackmail to enslave us, his lowly relations. What I couldn't understand was how Ethan got such bad grades when his head was full of so many facts.

I stared out the window, my mind seeking some sort of plan. How could we convince Tyler to take us? He thought we were a couple of annoying kids, so he wouldn't care about helping us. "We have to give him a reason to go," I said. "Something he can't refuse."

Ethan shrugged. "The only things he cares about are his trophies and his games."

I spun around. "Yes, that's it. Maybe there's something going on like a gaming event." I set the box on the desk and squeezed into the chair next to Ethan. My fingers flying across the keyboard, I began to search for events in WA DC. "There's a symphony," I read. "Classical music. There's a cat show. A bunch of plays. There's a geocaching event. There's a lecture by some doctor. There's—"

"Go back," Ethan said. Then he pointed to the

geocaching event. I clicked on the link. "It's a competition."

"What kind of competition?"

"Geocaching is like a treasure hunt. You use a
global positioning unit to find the treasures. Look,
it says anyone can enter but you need to be in a
team of two or more." And then we both said,
"There's a trophy!"

This had possibilities. Tyler pursued trophies
like a big-game hunter. I read farther down the
page, then groaned. "Crud! It was last week. We
missed it." I sank against the chair. It would have
been perfect. Luring Tyler with a trophy would
have been easier than luring a cat with tuna fish.
"Wait a minute, I know what to do." I pasted the
event's flyer into a new document, then changed
the dates to this week. "Ta-da!"

"The font doesn't match," Ethan pointed out.
"He'll notice."

"He won't notice if I do this . . ." I put the word
trophy into a huge bold font so it almost jumped off
the page. Then I snickered. "He won't notice anything else."

Gravel crunched beneath tires as Mom pulled

into the driveway. "We'll talk to him in the morning," I said, printing the flyer, then shoving it into my desk drawer. "I'll come over right after breakfast." Then I grabbed the box and hid it in the back of my closet, under my winter coat. I didn't want to leave it, but I knew it would be safe. Mom never asked me to clean my closet.

"When he finds out we changed the date, he'll kill us," Ethan warned as we headed downstairs and out the front door.

"He won't kill us."

"Then he'll do something worse." Ethan grabbed his bike handles. "He'll make us wash his underwear. *By hand*."

At that moment, I couldn't think of anything more disgusting. But it was a risk I was willing to take. Because that box was my birthday present and I was determined to open it.

Curiosity may have killed the cat but I was no cat.

7

JAX

Sunday

"Bye," I hollered as Mom backed the car out of the driveway. She was leaving early because Sunday was the busiest breakfast day at the Chatham Diner. She waved.

I ran upstairs to check on the metal box. It was still sitting in the back of my closet, underneath my winter coat. I gave it a little pat and said, "Don't worry, you'll be safe." I know it's weird to talk to a box. I'd checked it umpteen times during the night. I didn't usually worry about things getting stolen. Why was I so worried now?

After munching a couple handfuls of Cheerios, I jumped on my bike and rode to Ethan's. The streets were pretty empty. I passed a few joggers. The house where the two annoying dorkies lived was next. Dorkies are half dachshund and half Yorkie. They raced from their front porch, snarling like rabid hot dogs. "Oooh, I'm really scared," I taunted. "You guys are totally terrifying." They yapped and lunged, but I managed to swerve around them without causing an accident scene.

Ethan's neighborhood was so much nicer than mine. The houses were twice the size and the driveways were paved. His parents were just getting into their BMW when I reached the house. "Hi, Jax," Aunt Cathy said. She'd cropped her hair super short and wore a new pair of red glasses. Cathy was Mom's older sister and, from what I'd figured out, she'd been the "good" girl growing up while Mom had been the "difficult" girl. Cathy went to college and graduate school and got married, while my mom traveled and worked odd jobs and had a baby out of wedlock.

Uncle Phil tossed his briefcase into the car. He'd balded early so all he had left was a narrow strip of hair that wound around the back of his head.

But he was still pretty handsome—for an old guy. "What do you and Ethan have planned today?" He looked at me suspiciously.

"*Moi?*" I said with a shrug. "Just hanging out. Where are you going?"

"We're meeting some clients from China. They've developed a robotic toy dog. Unfortunately, they don't seem to care that it's Sunday." Aunt Cathy smiled. "Be sure to eat that barley salad I left in the fridge. It's healthy."

Sure, I'll eat the barley salad . . . if it's the very last edible thing left on earth.

As they drove away, I leaned my bike against the shed, then went into the house. Ethan was eating a bowl of cereal at the kitchen table. Tyler, wearing only a pair of boxers and socks, was standing in front of the refrigerator, staring at the shelves. "Hey, Tyler, whatcha doing?" I asked, trying to sound super cheerful. It's best to attract the wasp with honey, not vinegar, as the saying goes.

"Sustenance," Tyler mumbled. He splurted mustard onto a cold hot dog, then shoved half of it into his mouth.

"You can get sick if you don't heat those things," Ethan said. "You can get listeriosis."

"That's a super-duper interesting factoid," Tyler said before shoving the rest of the dog into his mouth, "However, what you didn't take into consideration is that this hot dog is soy, dipstick." He popped open an energy drink and chugged the whole thing. I hate that stuff. I'm bouncy enough without pouring caffeine and sugar down my throat.

Clearly my older cousin didn't care anything about his appearance. Though he had a somewhat cute face, it was covered in stubble and his nose was pimply. He didn't even bother to wipe the mustard drip from his boxers. And the socks had holes in the heels. "Well, nice chatting with you two dorks," he said, followed by a burp. "But I gotta get back to the campaign. We're designing a horde of invading Harpies to battle the Cyclops king." Tyler slammed the refrigerator shut.

And he called *us* dorks.

"Hey, Tyler," I said. "We have something to show you." I held out the flyer.

He glanced at it. "So?"

"We thought you might want to register. There's a trophy." I said the word *trophy* real slow. "You could probably win. I mean, how hard can it be?

You're the smartest guy I know." I almost gagged. Where was my pride? I was practically kissing his feet.

He took the flyer, his gaze scanning it with the quick-fire precision of a gamer. "Registration is tomorrow, in Washington, DC," he read. "Teams of two or more."

"Ethan and I talked it over," I said. "We can go as a team."

Tyler curled his upper lip. "You two?"

Ethan had been watching the conversation, his spoon held in midair, milk dripping down the handle. I elbowed him. "Uh . . ." He cleared his throat. We'd rehearsed this line last night over the phone. "You know Mom and Dad won't let you go with your friends. But they might let you go with us."

"The parental units are total drags about my friends." He scratched his fuzzy chin. "Does that mean you'll want to share the trophy?"

"It's all yours," I assured him. "We just want out of Chatham. It's so boring around here. We won't bug you once we get there. We'll pretend to be on your team but we can do something else. You don't even have to see us."

"I don't have to see you?" Tyler read the flyer again. "Okay, if you can convince the units, then I'm in. But I'm not paying for the gas and hotel."

"I bet Mom and Dad would pay," Ethan said.

"Then it's settled." He smashed the can and tossed it into the recycle bin. "Gather your field-trip permission forms, little dweebs. The quest for the geocache treasure will begin at dawn." He grabbed a loaf of bread, then strode out of the kitchen.

He didn't look like someone setting out on a quest, not with his buttcrack peeking out the top of his boxers.

"Correction," I whispered to Ethan. "The quest to open the *secret box* will begin at dawn."

8
ETHAN

Here are some interesting facts about toys: Twister was originally called Pretzel and the teddy bear was named after President Theodore "Teddy" Roosevelt, who liked to hunt bear. And Mr. Potato Head used to smoke a pipe but doesn't anymore because it's not politically correct.

I know these things because my parents own Rainbow Product Testing. Their specialty is children's toys. If someone invents a new toy for kids, the inventor can send it to Rainbow to make sure it's safe. They started the company when I was four years old. Dad was sick of teaching at the university and Mom was sick of staying at home, taking care of two boys. She said we acted like wild savages most of the time. I remember Tyler drawing a bull's-eye on my forehead with Mom's lipstick, then throwing things at me. I remember him convincing me to flush our entire supply of Costco toilet paper down the toilet until it wouldn't flush anymore and the bathroom became a lake. I remember the two of us taking all the food out of the refrigerator and putting it on the lawn to see how many raccoons showed up. Eight, as it turned out. And three dogs. Who could blame Mom for wanting to get away?

When a toy comes to Rainbow Product Testing, it first goes to the laboratory. The lab is my dad's territory. He holds a PhD in chemistry. The toy undergoes a series of tests to make sure it isn't made with toxic materials. No lead or radioactive leakage, no biological hazards that might make kids sick. Small parts have to be measured because they might cause choking. Kids eat toy parts all the time. I don't get that.

If the toy passes inspection, then it goes to my mom. She runs the marketing department. Mom has a master's degree in psychology. She helps the client figure out how to package the toy and decides the appropriate age group. Sometimes she brings in kids from the neighborhood to play and she observes them. She used to bring me and Tyler when we were younger, but she stopped bringing Tyler when she realized that he wasn't the same as other kids. He'd piece together a puzzle in less than a minute while the other eight-year-olds were still listening to the directions.

I pushed my bike into the lobby and leaned it against the counter. Since it was Sunday, there was no receptionist to tell me to put the bike outside. Jax had decided that it would be best for me to deal with my parents and she'd deal with her mom. She thought they might get suspicious if we presented ourselves as a team. She was probably right about that.

The lobby walls were covered with images of some of the famous toys my parents had worked with. As I walked toward the laboratory, I yawned. I'd had trouble falling asleep, not just because Tyler had beheaded Cyclopses all night, but because I was worried about Jax's latest plan. Tyler would eventually figure out that we'd changed the date on the flyer. And he'd make summer miserable for us. Well, for me, mostly. It's easier to retaliate if the victim's bedroom is right across the hall.

Whatever was in that metal box had better be amazing.

I put on a protective white smock and goggles before entering the lab. The lights were bright and the noise from the various machines made my head hurt. Dad was talking to the group from China. "We have complete facilities for both biological and chemical testing," he explained. "Our equipment includes soxhlet extractors, heating block digestors, ion chromatographers, and a flow injection mercury system." Dad waited for their translator to do her job, then he continued. "This allows us to test plastic, metal, paint, adhesives, fabric, and fillers, along with—" He noticed me and waved. "Excuse me for a moment," he told the guests. As the translator spoke to the group, Dad hurried over. "What's going on, Ethan?" he asked. "Is everything okay?"

"I need to talk to you about something."

"Is it an emergency?"

"No."

His expression relaxed. Who could blame him for feeling relieved? I hadn't been the easiest kid lately. There'd been a serious conversation a while back about making bad choices. Jax and I had gone to a movie and when it was over, she'd convinced me to sneak into another movie down the hall to see if her friends were inside. We got distracted by a car chase scene and got caught by a manager. Then we went to a sporting goods store and Jax talked me into riding double on a skateboard. We lost control, toppled a kayak, and crashed into a fishing pole display. Mom called a family meeting that night. Tyler suggested that I stop hanging out with Jax. Mom said we needed to be gentle with her. She said Jax made poor choices because she wanted attention. "It's not easy for a young woman to be without a father." Dad promised that he'd try to pay more attention to Jax. And I promised to speak up for myself more often. I could still hang out with her, but I didn't have to do everything her way.

I didn't do *everything* her way. Just most things. Look, if I didn't hang out with Jax I'd be totally alone most of the time. Or worse, I'd be stuck going to the movies with . . . my mother.

But there was something else. I went along with Jax because I figured she'd be safer with her loyal sidekick looking after her. She'd looked after me plenty of times. Like when, in the second grade, she'd knocked Jeremy Bishop off his feet because he'd been throwing dodge balls at me. And we weren't even playing the game.

"Would you like me to introduce you to our

guests?" Dad asked.

Whenever my parents introduced Tyler, there was always a long list of accomplishments that followed his name. "This is our son Tyler. He's a this and a that and he's won this and won that." But with me it's simply, "This is our son Ethan."

"No thanks," I said, staying next to the door. The sooner I got out of that noise, the better. I avoided my father's trusting eyes. "Jax and I want to go to Washington, DC, to help Tyler with a geocaching competition."

"Uh-huh." Dad reached out and fiddled with a beaker that was full of greenish fluid. Then he wrote something on a clipboard.

"So? Can we go?"

"Go?" He continued to write.

"Dad?" I asked. He got distracted easily.

"Oh, right. You and Jax want to go somewhere." He set the clipboard aside, then put a hand on my shoulder. "Is everything okay with Jax? It's been a few weeks since I checked in with her. Do you think she needs to talk about anything? Anything in particular? Boys, maybe?"

I cringed. Dad was trying to pay attention to Jax, just as he'd promised. But he never knew quite how to do it. He'd never once offered to talk to me about girls. And I was a year older than Jax. Did he think I was so shy I'd never get a girlfriend?

"Dad," I said. "Jax doesn't need dating advice. We want to go to Washington, DC."

The Chinese translator interrupted us. "Doctor Hoche, my employers have a few more questions for you."

"Yes, of course," Dad called. He adjusted his safety goggles. "Can you work this out with your mother? I'm okay with whatever she decides." Then he joined his clients.

After leaving the goggles and coat in the dirty laundry bin, I headed down the hall to find my mom.

Mom's section of the company was totally different from Dad's. No beakers here. Just a big bright room with tables and kid-sized chairs. When I was little, I usually sat in the green chair. Mom would sit in the corner, observing, taking notes. She never included me in her testing groups because if there were other kids around, I'd refuse to play with the toy and I'd hide under the table. So she'd bring me in alone. And she'd ask questions like, "Do you like the way the stuffed bear smells? Which color car do you like better?" She'd actually encourage me to taste the toys. For a long time, I thought all parents took notes while their kids played.

"Hey," Mom greeted. "I need your opinion."

She stood at a counter in her lab coat, a robotic dog perched in front of her. She handed me a remote control. "What do you think?" I pushed a button. The dog stood. I pushed another. The dog walked forward. I could make it sit and bark. I could even make it wag its tail. "Would you play with this?"

"I'm thirteen," I reminded her.

"Oh, so you're too old to play? That's the trouble with our society," she said, taking back the remote. "We think play is something only little kids should do. But it's just as important for adults—maybe more important." She tucked her short hair behind her ears. Even without her high heels, she was still taller than me. "So, what are you doing here?"

"Uh . . ." I could practically hear Jax's voice in my head. She'd made me memorize some of the lines. "Tyler wants to enter a contest and he said that Jax and I can be on his team. He said he'll drive." I held out the flyer.

"Geocaching?" She read the flyer. "It looks like fun but I'm confused. Why would Tyler want to take you and Jax? You don't exactly get along with him."

I pointed to the word *trophy*.

Mom smiled. "Oh, I see." She set the remote aside, opened a small fridge, and handed me a container of orange juice. "It all started with that first trophy in kindergarten. He built a working catapult out of Legos. The teachers couldn't believe it. They thought we'd helped but I assured them we hadn't. He did it all himself." She stopped abruptly. Then she smiled at me, her *other* son. "You made amazing things for the science fair too."

"Amazing?" I nearly snorted orange juice out of my nose. "I did the same potato electricity project five years in a row." Why? Because whenever the science fair rolled around, Tyler's experiment took over our house. Dad special-ordered supplies off the internet. Mom cleared the dining-room table, where Tyler toiled like a mad scientist. My parents always asked if I needed help with my project but I always said no. I could never compete with Tyler, so why try? I'd grab the old wires and a new potato. Kids started calling me Mr. Potato Head.

"Can we go to DC?" I asked.

"Hmmm." Mom pursed her lips. "How many nights?"

"We'll leave tomorrow morning and stay one night. That's it."

She slid her red glasses up her nose. "Did you ask your father?"

"He said it was up to you." I drank the rest of the orange juice. Mom hadn't made up her mind but the way her eyes were narrowed, I knew she was on the brink of a decision.

Jax's voice rang in my head. She'd come up with a pretty good argument. "Tyler's just going to sit in his room. This trip will get him out of his cave for a couple of days. Into actual sunlight."

Mom's eyes relaxed. "Sunlight? I didn't know his kind could venture out into sunlight. He'll need sunglasses."

"And sunscreen," I added. We both laughed.

"Okay, I'd better stop making fun of your brother. I think it's a great idea. It's summer and you need an adventure. And Tyler definitely needs a reason to get away from his computer." She smiled and kissed my cheek. "Okay. Tell your Aunt Lindsay that we'll cover the hotel and gas."

"Thanks," I said. Things were falling into place. Maybe everything would work out. We'd go to DC, the box would open, and Tyler would believe that the person in charge of the Geocaching contest had printed the wrong date on the flyer.

Maybe.

I tossed the empty juice container into the bin and headed for the door. But then I remembered something Jax had wanted me to ask. "Hey, Mom, who is Great-Aunt Juniper?"

Mom frowned. "How do you know about Juniper?"

I fiddled with the doorknob. "Well, Jax got a present in the mail and Aunt Lindsay took it away. Jax said the return address was Juniper Vandegrift. And Tyler said she's our great-aunt."

Mom sighed. "Look Ethan, just because a person is related to you by blood doesn't mean that person is family. Juniper is not someone you or Jax or Tyler need in your lives. She's not someone you should think about. "

"Did she do something wrong?"

"Her mistakes have nothing to do with you children. But please, don't bring this up with your Aunt Lindsay. It will only upset her. Just forget you ever heard the name Juniper." She hugged me. "Now go pack your bag for DC, and I'll make the hotel reservation. This will be a great way to start the summer."

As I stood outside Rainbow Product Testing, a familiar sensation tickled my nose. I leaned my bike against the building, then tilted my head back as the blood began to flow. Luckily it was a small bleed and stopped after a few minutes. The Kleenex I always kept in my pocket was all I needed.

I fished out my phone and called Jax. "I feel bad. We're lying about everything."

"We're not lying about *everything*," she said, the connection a bit fuzzy. "The part about going to DC isn't a lie. And the part about Tyler driving us and—"

"We're liars," I said, wiping my nostrils. "No matter how you try to spin it, Jax, we're lying."

"Do you see another way to figure out what's in the box?"

"Uh . . ." I said. "No."

"Stop worrying. It'll be fun. And you can have half of whatever's inside. But first we have to go to DC and open it."

"And then what?"

She chuckled. "If I had an answer for *Then what?* it wouldn't be an adventure."

9
JAX

When Mom works a long shift at the Chatham Diner, I cook for myself. Last summer I figured out how to make a cheese omelet. And I know how to dump fish sticks on a cookie sheet and shove them into the oven. I'm not much of a cook but I don't starve. That night I made spaghetti with olive oil and Parm cheese. Since I hate doing dishes, I ate right out of the pan. I didn't make anything green even though I know it's healthier to add a vegetable or two. Green is my least favorite flavor, except for pickles, which don't taste green.

There were two pieces of birthday cake left so I took one upstairs and ate it while sitting in my closet. I don't usually eat in my closet but the box was in there and, well, I liked looking at it. The metal was polished to a glossy sheen and perfectly smooth. And it was kinda warm to the touch. Maybe the heat came from a battery that kept the LCD screen working. That made sense. As I munched on cake I imagined what might fit inside. A piece of heirloom jewelry, a wad of cash, a treasure map?

When Mom got home, she barely had the energy to ask how my day was. She headed straight for the bathroom and filled the tub. I like hanging out with her while she takes a bath. I sit on the floor, a pile of beauty and fashion magazines in my lap. You can buy them for ten cents apiece from a big bin at the library. We laugh about the stupid things those people write about, like how to make your lips look plumper, or what kind of underwear makes your butt look smaller. This was our talking time.

"Mary's having gallbladder surgery," she told me as I settled on the floor. I set a fork and plate with the last piece of birthday cake on the edge of the tub. "I agreed to take her shift, which means I'll be doubling my hours this week. I'm sorry. I know this isn't the best way to start the summer." She pulled her long hair into a knot, then sank into the water.

Even though Mom worked all the time, we never seemed to have enough money. We'd always been renters, we'd always had an old car, we'd always clipped coupons. Aunt Cathy and Uncle Phil offered to help, but Mom refused. So Aunt Cathy used every holiday, even Bastille Day, as an excuse to give me gift cards. Hello? Bastille Day is celebrated in France.

"I was hoping we could go camping," Mom said as steam coated the mirror. We usually went camping the first week of summer vacation. "I'll see if your Aunt Cathy is planning any trips. Maybe you could go with her." She took a few bites of cake. Bathwater dripped off her hands, onto the plate.

"Actually, Ethan and Tyler are going to Washington, DC, to do this geocaching contest. I was hoping I could go with them." Did my voice sound innocent? Could she tell I'd planned the whole thing?

"What kind of contest?"

"Geocaching. It's a treasure hunt. The winning team gets a trophy."

She took another bite. "Is your aunt okay with this?"

"Yes," I said. "We already talked to her. She's going to pay for the hotel and gas. Tyler and Ethan are leaving in the morning. Can I go with them? It sounds like a lot of fun. And I'm not doing anything else. Besides, Ethan needs me. It will be crowded in DC and you know how he gets."

"It's so nice that you feel protective of your cousin." She licked frosting off her lips. "You were a baby the last time I visited DC. The cherry blossoms were beautiful. We went to the Lincoln Memorial. We . . ." She stopped speaking. Her brows pinched for a moment, as if fighting a headache. Was it a bad memory?

She finished the cake and set the plate on the corner of the tub. Then she closed her eyes and thought for a long while, the steady drip from the faucet the only sound. Her toes rested against a broken tile. I wanted to ask her about Great-Aunt Juniper. Why so many secrets? But she was tired and I didn't want to push things. And if I asked about my father, I'd just get the same response as always—*I've told you a million times, Jax, I don't know anything about him and I've forgotten his name.* So my nervous gaze flitted over a magazine advertisement for lipstick that never wore off, even if you ate a hamburger, even if you kissed. What was it made of—glue?

"You'll stay with your cousins?" Mom asked, turning to look at me.

"Yes," I said as I sat up straight.

"You won't get into trouble? Please, Jax, I really can't handle any more trouble right now. That candy-bar incident was very upsetting."

Candy Bar Incident. That sounded like the title of a novel. Yeesh.

"I won't get into trouble." I would do my absolute best to keep that promise. The last thing I wanted was to make my mom worry, or to disappoint her. She'd never have to know about the box or its contents. Life would return to normal as soon as I got back.

"Well then, it sounds like fun. I know you want to travel. There's a lot to see in DC." She closed her eyes again and sank deeper. "I love you, Jax."

"I love you too, Mom."

Neither of us mentioned the birthday box. We acted as if it never existed.

10
JAX

Monday

I didn't have to look out the window to know that the obnoxious person honking a car horn at eight in the morning was my cousin Tyler.

"Coming!" I hollered. Mom had already left for the diner. She'd tucked a twenty-dollar bill in my pocket. I ran across the lawn. The morning dew had already evaporated and a piercing blue sky promised a hot day. Good thing I'd chosen shorts. As I shoved my backpack into the trunk, Tyler honked again. Mr. Smith stood on his front porch in his pajama pants, glaring at Tyler's car. "Sorry,"

I called to him, then shut the trunk. Oops. I'd forgotten to return the stupid axe.

"Get in," Tyler barked. He hadn't combed his hair and his T-shirt was all wrinkled as usual.

"Jeez, you don't have to honk a million times. I heard you the first time. *Everyone in the universe heard you the first time.*" I scrambled into the backseat next to Ethan, who'd slid down so no one could see him.

"Your neighbor looks pissed," Ethan said.

"He always looks that way." Mr. Smith was the kind of person who complained about everything—the way we didn't mow our lawn, the way Mom left stuff hanging on the clothesline, the way our garbage cans stayed on the curb long after the garbage had been picked up. Putting his nose in our business was like his part-time job.

I set the metal box on the seat between me and Ethan. Tyler turned around. "Be sure to put on your seat belts. I promised Mom that I'd make sure you . . . Hey, is that the box you got at the garage sale?"

"Yep," I answered.

"Have you solved the puzzle yet?"

"Nope."

"You should take a reading in DC."

"Hey, that's a real good idea. I hadn't thought of that. Thanks." I smiled at Ethan.

Tyler's car was pretty nice. His parents drove it for a few years, then gave it to him when he turned sixteen. As we pulled away, Tyler honked again and waved at Mr. Smith. Ethan groaned and slid lower.

"Did you bring the measuring stuff?" I whispered.

"Uh . . . yeah. A protractor, a ruler, a pencil, the map . . ." Ethan paused for a moment. "I think that's all we'll need." He held on to a paperback book. His baseball cap was the same one he always wore, but instead of jeans, he was wearing plaid shorts. I'd almost chosen plaid shorts that morning. Thank goodness they were in the washing machine. Ethan and I didn't need to be matchy matchy.

I could barely sit still; every muscle in my body wanted to sprint. Today I'd push the button again and that would make me even closer to opening the box. "This is going to be fun," I blurted.

Tyler glanced at me in the rearview mirror. "Fun? This isn't a game, Jax. It's a serious quest.

There's a trophy at stake."

I had to stifle a giggle. *Quest* is such a gamer word. Tyler took things so seriously. I turned to ask Ethan if he'd brought any snacks, when weird music poured out of the back speakers—heavy drumming accompanied by a woman who was singing in a strange language. Correction, not singing—screeching as if being tortured. I wanted to plug my ears. The sound started to creep under my skin. "What is this?"

"It's the soundtrack from War Machine," Tyler said.

One of his games, Ethan mouthed.

"Don't you have any music that's good?" I asked.

"Good?" Tyler glared at me in the rearview mirror. "Define *good*."

"You know, like music the rest of the population listens to?" The screeching was joined by more female voices. A chorus of women in pain. I was in pain. "Anything. I'll even listen to country."

"For your information, little cousin, the *rest* of the population consists of mindless zombies who consume mainstream pop culture because they're brainwashed by the constant flow of commercials that convince consumers to buy anything no matter—oh look, there's Starbucks." He made a sudden turn off the road.

Thankfully, the music stopped when Tyler shut off the engine. He pulled a card from his wallet, one of the cards I'd given him as a bribe, then strode toward the coffee emporium's green doors. While we waited for him to get his mocha frappe triple shot whatever, I hatched the next part of our plan. "We should press the button as soon as we get to DC, but not in front of Tyler. I don't want to share it with him. Whatever's inside is for me and you. No one else."

"How are we going to get away from him?" Ethan asked. "Mom made him promise to watch us every second. She's worried we're going to get into trouble."

"We'll slip away when he goes to register for the competition." It sounded so easy.

"What if we can't figure it out?" Ethan fiddled with his book. "What if we can't get the box open?"

"Don't say that. We can figure it out. It will be attempt eight of ten. We'll still have two more tries." I set the box on my lap. "Besides, why would Juniper send a puzzle that's impossible to figure out? She wants me to open this. It's my birthday present."

Ethan glanced over at Starbucks. Tyler was still inside. "When he finds out he's a week too late for the competition, he's going to freak out."

I was used to Ethan's worrying but I was also used to calming him down. Stress wasn't good for him because it brought on nosebleeds. I cringed at the thought. "Tyler's always freaking out. We can deal with it. Besides, he can game in the hotel all night. Room service will bring him whatever he wants." I clutched the box. "This is so exciting. I can't stop thinking about what might be inside. Maybe it's some really expensive jewelry, like an heirloom. Or maybe a rare coin or a plane ticket for a trip to Paris. Do you think Juniper is rich?"

"I don't know," Ethan said. "But don't get your hopes up."

"Why not?"

"Because I hate it when you get your hopes up and then it doesn't work out. You get all sulky."

"I don't get sulky," I said. "When do I ever get sulky?"

"When do you get sulky?" Ethan pushed his baseball cap up his forehead. "Uh, last week when you thought that movie had opened and we went down to the theater and it wasn't playing and the rest of the day you were in the worst mood ever. And before that, when you didn't make the chess team and you locked yourself in your room and wouldn't come out. And—"

"Yeah, well I should have made that team. I'm good at chess." So maybe I sulked a little bit, but that's only because I don't like to be disappointed. Who does? It's so . . . disappointing.

Tyler opened the driver's door. He was wearing his favorite T-shirt, which read, *To Save Time Let's Assume I Know Everything*. He set his drink into the cup holder and started the engine. "Hey, Tyler," I asked loudly, over the music. "Do you know if Juniper is rich?"

"Nope." He backed the car out of the parking space.

"Do you know what kind of job she has?"

"Noooo." He pulled out of the parking lot.

I brushed my hand across the box's smooth, slightly warm surface. "Do you remember what she looks like?"

"Negatory."

"Do you remember anything about her?"

He headed toward the highway on-ramp. "Are you going to yap at me the whole way? 'Cause if you are, I would prefer the conversation to be about someone interesting. Like Marc Andreessen, inventor of the browser; or Elon Musk, SpaceX guy; or Bill Gates, all-around genius and master of the universe. Not some stupid old aunt who lives in Greece."

"Greece?" I leaned closer. "She lives in Greece? Are you sure?"

"That's what I remember."

I didn't have a Greek travel guide. I had one of Turkey, which was pretty close. I'd cut out a photo of a fishing village where you could rent a donkey to carry your stuff, then hike to a secluded white sand beach with water as blue as a Slurpee.

Did I finally have a relative living somewhere other than New Jersey?

Then I sighed, remembering that the return address on the package was for New Hope, Pennsylvania. "Do you know if—"

"Quiet," Tyler interrupted. "This is the good part." As he turned up the volume, a choir of screeching women, or perhaps they were birds, I really don't know, filled the car. The drumming was accompanied by the clang of clashing swords. Ethan and I were prepared. We pulled out our earbuds and stuffed them into our ears. Then I leaned my head against the window and watched the cars whizz by.

I imagined that if my dad had been around, he would have driven us to DC and Tyler would still be sitting in front of his computer. Dad and I would be buddies. He would have said to my mom, "Relax, Lindsay. Let Jax have some fun."

I don't normally notice cars but after we'd been driving for a while, a black car pulled up in the passing lane. It stayed there, right next to us, matching our speed for a really long time. "Pass already," Tyler grumbled. The car's windows were tinted so I couldn't see inside. I liked the silver jaguar that perched on the hood, as if ready to leap off. "Idjot," Tyler grumbled as the black car slowed and slid behind us.

About a half hour into our trip, Tyler stopped at a gas station. It was one of those big travel centers with the mini-market, bathrooms, and showers for truck drivers. While Tyler filled the tank, Ethan wandered over to a fruit stand and bought a bag of apples. I grabbed the metal box and followed.

We sat on a bench in the fruit stand's shade. Mom called Ethan's phone to check on me. I told her everything was fine. After handing the phone back to Ethan, I decided that if the box contained birthday money, I'd use it to buy myself a new phone.

Ethan wiped one of the bright red apples on his shirt, then handed it me. Juice ran down my hand as I took the first bite.

"That's a lovely box," someone said.

Both Ethan and I nearly jumped out of our shorts. We'd been looking in the other direction and hadn't noticed the two old people who'd walked right up to us. They stood very close, ignoring the whole personal space rule. Ethan immediately slid down the bench. He hates it when people get too close.

I'm not that good at telling how old someone is but the man looked older than God, with a totally bald head and a bunch of big brown splotches on his face. His mustache was perfectly trimmed, as if someone had drawn a white line above his lip, and his nose was real long—it reminded me of a beak. The woman's skin was much darker than his and her silver hair was knotted in a bun at the base of her neck. They were dressed in an old-fashioned way, as if going to church. He had a bow tie, and her floral dress reached to her ankles.

"That's a lovely box," the man repeated.

"Uh, thanks," I said, tossing my apple into the bushes. I gripped the box because they were both staring at it as if they wanted to eat it. Over at the pump, Tyler screwed on the gas cap, then went into the convenience store.

"That's a very interesting feature." The woman reached out to touch the screen but I hugged the box to my chest. She held her fingers aloft for a moment, her eyes widened, then she dropped her hand.

The man cleared his throat. "Where did you get it?"

"It was a present," I said, and suddenly I thought that maybe I was volunteering too much information. I mean, who were these people? Why did they care about my box?

The man wobbled a bit. That's when I noticed his cane. "It's so unusual. No seams. No hinges. How does it open?"

I looked at Ethan. He'd been very quiet but that was no surprise. A flash of understanding passed between us. Neither one of us wanted to talk to these two. We both rose from the bench. "Well, gotta go," I said.

"Wait." The woman's voice was so desperate-sounding that it stopped Ethan and me in our tracks. She smoothed her hair. "Would you be interested in selling it?"

Other than the fact that these people were a bit snoopy, I didn't have any reason to be worried. But an uncomfortable feeling settled over me, as if I'd been cornered and needed to get away. Why did I feel like this? They were so old, surely they couldn't hurt me. I hugged the box to my chest. "Why would you want to buy my box?"

The man's gaze drifted up to my eyes. Though he smiled, it was cold and forced. He leaned on his cane. "Allow me to introduce myself. I am Mr. Hatmaker and this is my wife, Mrs. Hatmaker. We own a store called . . . Peculiarities. We specialize in unique pieces of folk art." The woman continued to stare at the box. "We travel around and buy odd items. And that box is odd indeed."

"Oh," I said. I guess it made sense that they'd be interested in my box. But the way he was smiling made me shudder. The smile was frozen in place, as if he wanted me to inspect his teeth.

Mrs. Hatmaker's finger trembled as she pointed. "What about the little screen? Does it do something special?"

"Not really," I said. Their questions were boring. Besides, I wanted to get a candy bar before we hit the road again. "Well, nice talking to you." I tugged on Ethan's sleeve and was about to walk away when Mr. Hatmaker's eyes widened.

"We'll pay you two hundred dollars," he said.

My mouth fell open. "Huh?"

"Three hundred dollars." He took out his wallet. I was about to say no when Mrs. Hatmaker offered five hundred dollars.

Ethan gasped.

"Wait a minute," I said. "You'd pay five hundred dollars for this box?"

"It's very . . . peculiar," Mr. Hatmaker said. He pulled out five bills and offered them to me. Maybe they did this all the time. Maybe five hundred dollars was no big deal to the owners of a shop called Peculiarities. But it was a big deal to me. I'd never had that much money.

But something felt wrong—very wrong. I hugged the box tighter. "This is a family box," I said. "I can't sell it. Thanks anyway."

As Ethan and I walked away, the Hatmakers started to argue with each other, their voices carrying across the parking lot.

"We can't let it go," Mrs. Hatmaker pleaded.

"Calm down, Martha."

"How can I calm down? I can feel it. I can sense its presence."

"Control yourself. Don't make a scene."

I glanced over my shoulder as Mr. Hatmaker grabbed his wife's arm and yanked her away. They got into a black car with tinted windows and drove off, taking their five hundred dollars with them. Mom could have used that money. Had I made the wrong decision not selling the box?

No, I couldn't second-guess myself. I'd come this far to find out what was inside. I was going to see it through.

"Five hundred dollars," Ethan said. "Can you believe it? You know, after you get whatever's inside, you can always sell the box."

Clearly, carrying around such an unusual box had attracted unwanted attention. I didn't want anyone else to ask questions, so I opened the car door and set the box on the back floor, covering it with my purple coat. Ethan tossed the bag of apples inside. After making sure Tyler hadn't left the keys in the ignition, we locked the doors and walked toward the convenience store.

"Those people were weird. Did you see how she was breathing? She was panting like a dog," I said.

"She's old. She's probably got emphysema or something."

"And her fingers kept twitching. I thought she was going to grab it."

"She probably has Parkinson's," Ethan said. "It makes you tremble and shake."

But something wasn't right. "They didn't get gas," I said, stopping in my tracks. "They pulled their car into the station but they didn't get gas. They just talked to us."

"Maybe they just wanted to go to the fruit stand."

"They weren't carrying any fruit and they had plenty of money to buy some." Weird.

"Money is clearly not an issue," Ethan said. "They were driving a brand-new Jaguar. Those cars are expensive."

"A Jaguar? Did it have a silver jaguar on the hood?"

"Uh . . . yeah."

I didn't know what to make of this information. Of course it was a coincidence. What else could it be? My stomach growled. I looked back to make sure the creepy old Hatmakers were definitely gone, then went into the store.

Tyler had found an old-fashioned pinball machine at the back. As he flipped the levers, lights flashed and a bell chimed. Lost in another game, he'd forgotten all about us.

I got a Snickers bar. Ethan grabbed a bag of chips and some mini doughnuts. After we'd paid, we headed out the door. Tyler caught up to us. "Did you go pee-pee?" he asked us in a baby voice.

Ethan turned red. "Oh that's real funny. We're not little kids, Tyler. You don't have to ask us if we peed."

"Yeah, well I'm the chaperone on this trip. So pee now or hold it until we get there, little bro." He stopped. "What the . . . ? My car!"

I dropped the Snickers bar and gasped.

11
ETHAN

FACT: *The average American eats sixty-three doughnuts a year. That's a little more than one a week, which doesn't seem like a lot to me. The box I'd just bought at the convenience store had six mini doughnuts. I'd eat them every day if I could. Mom never buys doughnuts. She's waging a battle against anything deep-fried.*

Just as I opened the box of minis, Tyler started yelling. Who was he yelling at? Wait. Why was there glass on the ground?

It was gone. I knew it was gone before Jax yelled at Tyler to unlock the doors. I knew it before she reached in, before her face turned as pale as the moon. Before her eyes welled with tears.

"They took it," she cried. "They took my box!"

There were no other people around. Ours was the only car at the pump and the fruit stand guy was plugged into headphones, reading a magazine. Tyler stood absolutely still, his mouth halfway open, staring at the bits of safety glass that dangled down the side of the car door. Someone had broken the back passenger window. I didn't know what to do.

A red truck pulled up to the opposite pump. The driver got out and glanced at our window. "Tough luck," he said. Then he began to fill his tank.

"If they took my music I'm going to freak!" Tyler climbed into the driver's side and searched through his stuff. Then he emerged, his GPS unit in hand. "Everything's there," he said with a puzzled look.

I searched the trunk. My backpack lay next to Jax's. "Everything's here, too."

Tyler threw his hands in the air. "So why'd they break the window if they didn't take anything? What was the objective?"

"Hello?" Jax said. "Aren't you listening to me? They took my box!" She ran toward the sidewalk and frantically looked up and down the street.

"Who cares about your stupid box?" Tyler said, running a hand through his messy hair. "When Mom sees this window, she's going to kill me."

He'd had the car for only a couple of months and he'd already dented the back fender and broken a front headlight. Yeah, Mom was going to kill him. But Tyler's fate didn't worry me. It was Jax who worried me. She paced up and down the sidewalk, her fists balled up, her face flaming. She'd sulk for weeks over this. We'd talk about nothing else. It would be even worse than the time she lost that lottery ticket, the one she'd been sure was a winner. We'd retraced her steps for days but never found it.

"Jax," I called. "You can't do anything. They're gone."

The cashier stuck his head out the convenience store door. "You want me to call the police?"

"Yes," Tyler said. "Request immediate assistance. Thanks."

Jax ran back to our car, her ponytail coming undone. "We can go after them." She brushed glass shards off the passenger seat, then scrambled in. "Let's go. Hurry!"

"What are you talking about?" Tyler asked. "We don't know who did this."

"Yes we do," she said. "It was those two old people. I know it was them!"

Could it have been the Hatmakers? But they were ancient. Old people don't break car windows. "We watched them drive away," I pointed out.

"Well they came back, broke the window, and stole my box."

I peered into the car. Jax was getting all worked up, clutching the front seat, her hair hanging in her face. I tried to be the voice of reason. "We can't follow them. We need to stay and talk to the police."

"But they're getting away," she insisted. "Let's go!"

How could I get through to her? She always did things without thinking about the consequences—it was her modus operandi. Was that my sidekick role, to constantly warn her of danger? If this were a comic book, I'd be called Caution Boy.

"We can't leave the scene of a crime," I told her as I tossed the bag of chips and the box of doughnuts into the front seat. Early that morning, Mom and Dad had called a family meeting to discuss what to do if we got lost, what to do if we got a flat tire, and what to do if we got into an accident. Wait. For. Police. "The insurance company won't cover the repairs unless we file a report." I knew this because we'd been in an accident before. Some uninsured guy had rear-ended us at a four-way stop. "Maybe the police will catch the Hatmakers and get the box back." I tried to sound hopeful.

"Hatmakers? Who are the Hatmakers?" Tyler asked.

Jax climbed back out and stood with her hands planted on her hips. "Okay, listen carefully. *This is important.* The Hatmakers are two old people we were talking to over by the fruit stand. They wanted to give me five hundred dollars for the box."

"Are you saying that two old people broke my car window just so they could get your box?" Tyler asked.

"Yes, that's what I'm saying, so let's go find them," Jax urged. "That box was my birthday present."

"Hey, you said you got the box at a garage sale." Tyler folded his arms and glared at Jax. "I'm sensing some deleted details. Reboot and try again."

The pause was a long one. I could practically hear Jax's brain calculating the risks. Was she going to tell him the truth—that the box was supposed to be returned to sender but we took it? If he knew, he'd have blackmail power over Jax until she gained blackmail power over him.

She groaned. "Where I got it doesn't matter. What

matters right now is that it was stolen." She turned to me. "Can you search their name?"

"Sure." I took out my phone and typed HATMAKER. "There are over two hundred people named Hatmaker in the United States, but none around here," I said.

"He called her Martha. Try that."

"No match."

Tyler rolled his eyes. "Gee, Sherlock, you think a couple of thieves are going to give you their *real* names?"

"Police are on the way," the clerk announced as he walked toward us, a broom in his hand. "Hey, could you move your car? I've got customers waiting to use the pump."

As the clerk swept away the glass, Tyler moved the car from the fuel pump to a parking spot in front of the convenience store. Then we waited. And waited. I guess a broken car window and a stolen box wasn't high priority on the police department's agenda. Jax went into sulk mode, her lips pursed, her arms folded tightly, not saying a word. I read my book. Tyler called his friend Walker and they argued about the color of Cyclops blood. Time passed. I don't mind silence. I can sit for hours happily not saying anything. But when Jax doesn't talk, it means she's thinking. "Are you planning revenge?" I asked her.

"Maybe."

I could appreciate the desire. It still stung whenever I remembered how Jeremy Bishop stole my Pokémon cards in the third grade.

"Hey," Jax suddenly blurted. "Those Hatmakers said they owned a shop. What was it called? Oddities? Weirdities? What was it?"

"Peculiarities," I remembered.

"Yeah, that's it. Look it up." She nudged my elbow. I searched and found a shop called Peculiarities in Los Angeles. But the website showed a photo of the owner—a young woman named Nelson. Jax leaned against the car, her mood going sour again. I felt bad for her. She'd never know what our mysterious great-aunt had sent.

When the police finally arrived, Jax gave a description of the Hatmakers. She remembered little details that I hadn't noticed, like the way they wore their hair, and the color of their clothes. I didn't say much. The officer kept trying to trip Tyler up by asking the same questions over and over. Did he think my brother broke the window and was blaming it on someone else? Did he think we were all lying? Just because we were kids, that didn't mean we were trying to get away with something.

Uh, scratch that. We *were* trying to get away with something.

When Jax described the puzzle box, she said nothing about our great-aunt or how the box was supposed to have gone back to the post office. "It's a metal box, very shiny, with an LCD screen on the top and a button on the side. If you find it, please don't push the button. Seriously." She pointed to the officer's notepad. "Write that down."

"What will happen if I press the button?"

"You'll ruin everything," Jax said.

He removed his glasses. "What, *exactly*, will I ruin?"

Jax didn't answer. She looked at me. I'd been standing on the other side of the car, hoping to avoid the officer. I took a deep breath. "Uh . . . the box is a puzzle," I said, focusing my gaze on the officer's nose. Because sometimes I don't know if I should look into a person's right eye, or the left eye, or flit between the two. "My parents own a toy-testing company, so we get all sorts of fun stuff."

"A puzzle, huh? Okay, that's all I need." The officer handed Tyler a card. "Your parents can contact me at this number and I'll send them a copy of the report. It'll take a few days to process."

"Do you think you'll find my box?" Jax asked, her face clenched.

He adjusted his sunglasses. Sweat dotted his upper lip. It had to be super hot in that polyester uniform. At least the UPS guys got to wear shorts. "Honestly, kid, I wouldn't count on it."

As the police car drove away, Jax flicked a piece of glass off the car's window ledge. "They won't do anything. They think it's just a stupid box."

"Well it is just a stupid box," Tyler said. "Why don't you two care about my car? All you talk about is that box. Look. At. My. Car. How are we going to drive to DC like this?" He took out the back floor mat and shook it. "Don't stand there like you've just seen Medusa. Start cleaning."

"Medusa?" Jax asked.

"Greek Mythology One-Oh-One," Tyler said. "Jeez, how can you not know about Medusa? She turns people into statues. She's on level two of Cyclopsville, right next to the Furies." He set the floor mat back.

Furies? Jax mouthed.

"Don't ask," I whispered.

Now that the box was gone, Jax and I had no reason to go to DC. Maybe we could avoid the whole fake geocache contest and never have to admit that we'd lied. "Uh, we can't drive all the way to DC with a broken window," I said. "It's dangerous and Mom will flip out. We should go home."

"I'm not going home," Tyler said. "I set out on a quest and I'm going to get that trophy. I can fix this window." After making that statement, he stared at the empty hole that used to be a window.

Here's the thing about my brother—he's a genius on paper, and he can solve any math or computer problem under the sun, but ask him to fix something and he's useless. If he got stranded in the desert and the only way back to civilization was to change the flat tire on his car, we'd find his vulture-pecked skeleton weeks later. My dad's the same way. If you need an analysis of fibers in your breakfast cereal he'll type up a report and get it to you the following morning, but if the toilet lever is sticking, forget about it.

"I've been thinking," Jax whispered. She pulled me away from the car and Tyler's ears. "What if those Hatmakers push the button? What if they waste the last three readings and don't figure out that it's a puzzle? The box will go to waste!" Her eyes widened. "Or what if they do realize it's a puzzle and they get the eighth reading and the ninth reading and draw the circles like we did?"

"Then they'll go to the right spot," I said, immediately regretting my words, because as I said them, an idea lighted up Jax's eyes.

"We can ask Juniper."

"Huh?"

"Yeah. We can go to her house. It's her puzzle box. She must know where it opens. She can tell us and we can go to the right spot and wait for the Hatmakers to show up."

"No way. We're supposed to forget we heard Juniper's name, remember? And you want to see her in person?"

"There's something going on here, I know it. Something beneath the surface. I can feel it." By this time, Jax and I were in a huddle next to the convenience store door. People were coming and going, carrying bags of chips and sodas. "Whatever is inside that box, it belongs to me. It wants to be with me."

I frowned. "What are you talking about? The box *wants* to be with you? That sounds crazy." Tyler was trying to cover the window with his coat, but it wasn't working.

Jax stuck out her lower lip. "Ethan, this is really important."

"Oh no, I'm not falling for that." I reached into my back pocket and pulled out my wallet. "Look Jax, your birthday present was stolen. I'm sorry, but it's gone. Sometimes you have to let things go." I walked into the store and bought a box of plastic wrap and some duct tape. While Tyler watched, I covered the window with two layers of wrap, securing it around the edges with the tape. It wouldn't earn me an engineering degree but it was functional. I threw the leftovers into the trunk.

"Cool," Tyler said as he checked out the new window.

Jax grabbed my arm and began whispering again. "We need to get Tyler to take us to Juniper. We'll have to tell him the truth."

"Uh . . . I'm not telling him the truth," I said, shaking my head. "No way. I'm not suicidal."

"Then I'll tell him." She cleared her throat. "Tyler, I have something to tell you."

"What?" he asked.

"Uh-oh," I murmured, putting some space between us.

My brother's temper is like a flash flood. Flash floods take people by surprise. Survivors have reported that they were standing in a dry riverbed and suddenly found a wall of water rushing at them, sweeping everything away. When Tyler was little, he'd throw himself on the grocery-store floor and kick and scream. Sometimes he threw things or kicked things. Mom called his outbursts temper tantrums. Dad said Tyler needed to grow up and act like a man.

Jax had seen Tyler's temper. So she knew what she was in for.

She folded her arms and looked him right in the eye. "There is no geocaching contest. It was last week."

Tyler cocked his head, his expression remaining calm. "What did you just say?"

"We changed the date on the flyer so you would take us to Washington, DC."

"You changed the date?" His neck tensed.

"Yes." Jax stepped back. We both saw it at the same time, that look in his eyes. The rage was right there, boiling in his brain, ready to spill forth.

"Here we go," I whispered. During a flash flood, it's a good idea to hold on to a tree. During a Tyler tantrum, the best thing is to evacuate the premises. But what was I going to do, run across the parking lot and hide behind the fruit stand?

"Changed the date?" Spit flew out of his mouth. His eyes blazed, his breathing came fast and shallow.

"Let me get this straight. You told me there was a geocaching contest and there's no geocaching contest? Just because you wanted a ride to Washington, DC?"

Jax fiddled with the hem of her shirt. "Yeah but—"

He shot a deadly look at me. "You knew about this?" I nodded. Why did he seem taller all of a sudden? And was he frothing at the corners of his mouth? "Do you know what you've cost me?" More spit. "I'm in the middle of developing the fourth level of Cyclopsville. You peons have wasted an entire day of work. *And* my car was vandalized. Vandalized!" With a sweep of his arm, he dismissed us, got into the car and slammed the door. All four doors clicked into lock mode. The engine roared to life.

"Wait. Tyler, listen." Jax knocked on the driver's window. Tyler's hands gripped the steering wheel. "Juniper sent that box to me for my birthday." The car chugged as Tyler put it into reverse. "She wanted me to solve the puzzle but I couldn't do it alone. I needed your help!"

He backed out of the parking spot, then turned onto the road and picked up speed, the tires squealing as if they were also pissed. And then he was gone. I had to give my brother some credit—he'd really showed self-control this time. No punching holes, no throwing food. Dad would have been proud.

Jax pushed a lock of hair from her eye. "He's not really leaving us, is he?"

"I told you not to tell him," I said. Why doesn't anyone listen to Caution Boy? I sighed and walked over to the fruit-stand bench. Jax watched the road for a bit longer, then sat next to me.

"He'll come back," she said. But then she scrunched up her face. "Won't he?"

"He'll come back. He just needs to burn off some steam."

My brother wasn't my favorite person. He was rude and arrogant. He never showed any interest in what I was doing and often acted as if I didn't exist. But he wasn't stupid. Abandoning his brother and twelve-year-old girl cousin at a gas station would not go over well with the parents.

Sure enough, ten minutes later, the car pulled back into the lot and screeched to a stop right at our feet. Tyler got out. His eyes narrowed as he stared down at us.

"Tell me more about that box."

12
JAX

I told Tyler everything. How the package had arrived on my birthday, how Mom had grabbed it and how she'd thrown it into the car, forbidding me to have it. I told him how Ethan and I had followed Mom to the diner and how I'd intercepted the package from Michael the breakfast cook. How we'd opened it in the park, pressed the button five times, then went to Tyler's room to get help, where he pushed it the sixth time. "After you explained the geometry, we took the train and did the seventh reading. The right spot is either in Lake Oneida or in Washington, DC. I figured Juniper wouldn't make me stand in the middle of a lake so we tricked you into taking us to DC."

Tyler listened, his arms tightly folded. But he didn't look at me the whole time I was talking. Just kept staring over my head. Ethan had slid to the end of the bench. I know he wasn't afraid of Tyler punching him, or anything like that, but Ethan doesn't like confrontation. He's sensitive that way. I'm different. If Tyler yelled at me, I'd yell right back. Maybe that was why Ethan and I got along so well—we were opposites.

"I couldn't get to DC without your help," I explained. "That's why I lied to you. I was worried you'd blackmail me. It was my idea, not Ethan's. I'm sorry." I tapped my feet, anxiously waiting for his reaction.

A car pulled into the station, another drove away. I could picture those stupid Hatmakers. Were they laughing about their great find? About how they'd sell the box in their shop? The box's smooth, warm surface was still fresh against my fingertips.

"It doesn't make sense." Tyler narrowed his eyes and kept staring into space. "Why would Juniper send the box to *you*? I'm the brains in the family. She should know that. There've been six articles about me in the Chatham newspaper." This wasn't the reaction I'd expected. He didn't seem angry—more like *insulted*.

"I don't know why Juniper sent the puzzle box to me," I said. "But she did and here we are." A wave of frustration rolled over me. It felt as if we'd been at that stupid gas station for days! "Why did I leave it in the car? I had a bad feeling about those people. You should never ignore a bad feeling. Never." I usually listened to my instincts but I'd let myself down.

Tyler scratched his five-o'clock-shadowy chin. "I'm the one who figured out how to solve the puzzle. So I'm the one who should get to open the box, not those hat people."

"Hatmakers," Ethan quietly corrected.

"Whatever. The point is, this great-aunt of ours made a huge mistake sending the box to you. If she'd sent it to me, it would already be opened. And whatever is inside would be sitting on my shelf, next to my trophies."

I should have been insulted. In Tyler's universe, his intellect reigned supreme. But a little ray of hope appeared. Maybe my "quest" wasn't over. "Tyler?" I said as sweetly as possible. "It's obvious that Juniper doesn't know you are the genius in the family. If we go and see her, you can tell her that she made a mistake sending the box to me. She lives nearby." I pulled a folded piece of paper from my pocket. It was the corner of the packaging with Juniper's return address.

"Yes," he said, nodding slowly. "She should be informed." He slid back into the driver's seat.

"Wait, what are we doing?" Ethan asked.

"This long lost aunt of ours needs to send all future puzzles to me," Tyler announced.

I broke into a huge grin. Who cared about *future* puzzles? I only cared about this one. Nobody steals a birthday present from Jax Malone without a fight. "Woo-hoo!" I cried.

Ethan sat very still, his face tight with uncertainty. I knew he was coming up with all sorts of reasons why we shouldn't do this. I could practically see them streaming through the air. I sat next to him at the end of the bench. "We aren't expected home until tomorrow night. Everything will be okay," I told him.

"What if she doesn't want to see us?" he asked.

"Why wouldn't she want to see us?"

"Because something happened and she's not

welcome in the family." Ethan chewed on his lip. "Maybe she doesn't like us as much as our parents don't like her." It was a reasonable excuse, but I was better at arguing. I was going to join the debate team as soon as I got into high school.

"If Juniper didn't want to see us then she wouldn't have sent me a birthday present," I pointed out. "And she wouldn't have included her return address." I waved the piece of paper. "She'll tell us the exact spot where the box opens. Then we'll thank her and we'll still have time to get to Washington, DC, and stay in the hotel like we're supposed to."

"And then what?" Ethan asked.

"Then we'll find those Hatmakers and demand the box back," I said. I knew it wouldn't be that easy but what else could I do? I'd never wanted anything this much in my life. "Come on, Ethan, it'll be okay. What else are you going to do? Go home and read?"

Ethan grumbled something under his breath, then he slowly walked to the car and slid into the backseat. He never stayed mad at me for long. I wasn't worried.

As soon as I'd climbed into the front passenger

seat and closed the door, Tyler smirked at me. A deal was about to be made.

"When the quest is concluded, I'll tell my parents that we got the dates wrong for the geocaching competition and that no one was to blame on one condition."

This was expected. Tyler never did anything for free. "What's the condition?"

"That if we get the box back and if whatever's inside is worth a lot of money, then we sell it and I get half. I'm saving for a new gaming mouse."

"Half?" I gulped. "But I promised half to Ethan."

He snorted. "Why would you split it with Ethan? You own the box, I've got the brains. What's Ethan's role in all this?"

"Ethan's role is . . ." I paused, glancing over the seat. Ethan was slumped down low, his book propped in front of his face. "He's . . ." Ethan raised his eyebrows and looked at me over the top of the book. "He's my best friend and he fixed the window," I said. "And I already promised half to him."

"I'm okay with thirds," Ethan said.

"Thirds it is." Tyler smacked his hand on the steering wheel. "The quest to retrieve the secret box has commenced."

As Tyler drove away from the gas station, Ethan gave me that look I knew so well—the *what are you getting me into* look. I smiled at him. "Don't worry. This is the *Then what?* part of the adventure. Remember?"

13
ETHAN

FACT: *Alexander Graham Bell, the inventor of the phone, thought we should answer by saying "Ahoy." It was Thomas Edison who suggested "Hello." That's a pretty cool fact.*

Another fact: The first mobile handheld phone was invented way back in 1973. It weighed two and a half pounds and had only thirty minutes of battery life. In those days Google didn't exist. If you needed to do research, you had to go to the library. The actual building. And if you needed a map, you had to go to a store or gas station and buy one. An actual paper map. Thanks to my new phone, it was easy to get driving directions to Juniper's house.

I typed the return address, which was in New Hope, Pennsylvania, and waited for the map to appear on the screen. Mom and Dad gave me the phone after I'd brought up my grade in English from C plus to B minus. My parents want me to get better grades. They never have grade discussions with Tyler, Mr. 4.2. But I get the lecture about once a month. "We know you're capable of doing more," they always say. "We just want you to do your best. That's all we ask."

What if my best is a B minus? Would the world come to an end?

There are all sorts of accolades for people who get As—clubs, awards, honors, scholarships, even trophies. But nothing is given to the B people. Statistically, there are more B people in this world than A people, but that argument never flies with my parents.

I'm not sure what my problem is, exactly. I read more than anyone I know, and the facts all stick to my brain like fruit flies to honey. But when I sit down to take a test I get nervous and start second-guessing myself. Mom says introverts often lack confidence. Dad says that some people aren't wired to be test takers. Tyler says I'm stupid.

I scanned the New Hope tourist site. "New Hope lies on the Delaware River," I said from the backseat. Jax was sitting in the front seat. "It's the longest free-flowing river in the Eastern US. It starts in the Catskill Mountains and goes three hundred thirty miles to Delaware Bay. About five percent of the US population relies on it for drinking water. And—"

"How about giving us a factoid break?" Tyler said.

I sighed and finished the sentence in my head. *And it is fed by two hundred sixteen tributaries.*

Jax said something to Tyler, but I didn't catch it. The atmosphere had changed and I'm not talking about the weather. When I'd asked Jax why she was sitting up front, she'd said it was because she couldn't see very well through the plastic-wrap window. Maybe that was true but it felt like she'd deserted me. This had started as Jax and my adventure, but now we were splitting the prize with Tyler.

"Estimated time of arrival?" Tyler asked.

"We should be there by ten o'clock," I grumbled. Jax turned around and looked at me.

"What's the matter?"

"Nothing." I folded my arms and slid down in the seat. Guess sulking ran in our family.

Jax was squirming. She fixed her ponytail, then

squirmed some more. When Tyler reached to turn on his music, she poked Tyler's arm. "How come our great-aunt lived in Greece?"

"I don't know."

"Where do you think she got such a weird box? Did she stick the LCD screen into it or did it come that way? Is she married? Do we have a great-uncle too? Did she—?"

"What is this, Twenty Questions? Didn't you Google her?" Tyler asked as if we were too stupid to think of that. Jax darted around and looked at me, wide-eyed. *Google*, she mouthed. Then she glared at me as if it was my fault we hadn't done a search.

I wasn't about to admit to my brother that we had failed to do something so obvious. "We already did," I told him. Jax watched hopefully as my fingers flew across the phone.

"And . . . ?" Tyler asked.

I held the phone low so he couldn't tell what I was doing. "And what?" I stalled.

"And what did you find? Jeez, are we speaking the same language? Maybe I should try Pig Latin. Atwhay idday ouyay indfay?"

"I found . . ." I tried another search engine. Juniper Vandegrift didn't appear anywhere. "I found . . . I found nothing." I sat back against the seat and looked into Jax's eyes. "It's really weird but absolutely nothing comes up. Not a birth date, not an address, not a Facebook page. It's almost as if she doesn't exist."

Jax frowned. "But she does exist. She sent me a package."

"Widen the search," Tyler said. "Birth records, college alumni associations, phone book records— she's there."

"She's not here," I insisted.

"Then she's living under an alias, or she's paid someone to remove her records," Tyler said. "If she doesn't want to be found then it's possible the return address is fake."

"Fake?" Jax said. "But it can't be fake. I have to find that box."

Tyler followed my directions off the interstate. The scenery changed quickly. No more fast-food restaurants or strip malls. Everything was green and lush and in full bloom.

"Wow, the people around here must be rich," Jax said as we passed sprawling estates with manicured lawns and huge winding driveways. "Do you think Juniper is rich? She must be if she lives out here.

Really rich." I could tell that Jax was building a huge story in her head about our great-aunt, just like the stories she'd built about her father. Hopefully, reality wouldn't be too disappointing.

We passed old stone buildings and smaller houses from the early colonial period. You see a lot of those around here. A few turns in the road and we passed a *Welcome to Historic New Hope* sign. Tyler pointed out that my estimated time of arrival was off by sixteen minutes.

New Hope was a weird place. Every other shop looked like an art gallery of some sort. There was a tie-dyed T-shirt shop, a bunch of craft stores, and a store that sold healing stones. A bunch of Harley Davidson motorcycles were parked in front of a stand selling roasted turkey legs. "Hey," I said, pointing. "That's a medieval gallery." A full-sized coat of armor hung in the window.

"Cool," Tyler said. He slammed his foot, stopping right in the middle of the road. I was thrust forward against my seat belt. The car behind us honked, its brakes screeching.

"Whoa," Jax complained, bracing herself against the dashboard. "What'd you do that for?"

"See any swords?" Tyler asked.

Tyler had a sword collection that wasn't allowed to leave his bedroom. Mom said someone might get hurt, even though the blades were dull because they were replica productions from some of his favorite movies. He had Glamdring, Gandalf's sword, and Excalibur, King Arthur's sword, and Luke Skywalker's lightsaber, to name a few. Actually, I think Mom was more worried about people making judgments. She wasn't trying to protect Tyler—everyone already knew he was a geek. I think she was protecting her own reputation. Her job was to make sure toys were safe, so she was totally opposed to toy weapons.

"No," I lied, rubbing the back of my neck. "I don't see any swords." The car behind honked again.

We drove a bit farther, until we reached West Ferry Street. "There's a spot," Jax announced, pointing. It was a perfect spot, plenty of room, between a Chevy truck and a Volvo station wagon. Tyler slowed, eyed the space for a moment, then passed by.

"Not enough room," he said.

Jax scowled. "But there was plenty of—"

"Not enough room," Tyler repeated.

I tapped Jax's shoulder. "Remember what I told you." After flunking the parallel-parking section of the driving test, Dad had tried to explain the technique in mathematical terms. Tyler had gotten so frustrated he overturned his cereal bowl and stomped out of the kitchen. It was a sensitive subject.

Tyler drove around the block, twice, then found a space in a church lot that didn't require parallel parking. Even though it was hot out, Jax grabbed her purple coat and slipped it on. She'd found it at a garage sale and had talked the woman into selling it for $1.50. She loved that coat because it sparkled. I can't say I've ever loved a piece of clothing. I don't even care what I wear, so long as it's comfortable and not sparkling purple. I used to wear hoodies, but Mom said I was always hiding beneath the hood. So she banned them. Then I got the baseball cap and even though I wear it every day, she hasn't complained. Yet. The brim shades me from the sun, and from people who try to look into my eyes when talking to me.

We had to walk a couple of blocks to Ferry Street. "We're here," I said, checking the map on my phone. We stopped on the sidewalk, across the street from a bunch of identical houses. They were row houses—individual houses that share walls. A factoid popped into my head. The Europeans developed row houses in the sixteenth century as a way to fit more people into smaller spaces. I didn't share that info, however.

It would have gone unappreciated in this group.

"Juniper's address is the one on the end," Jax said.

While the other porches were decorated with flowerpots, the last porch was bare. And the curtains were closed. Was Juniper the person who lived in that house? A person who'd erased all her records from the internet. A person who'd been evicted from our family. A person we weren't supposed to think about.

Just then, Tyler's phone rang. "Is it Mom?" I asked, my heart doubling its pace. What would we tell her?

"It's Walker," Tyler said reading the screen. "Hey, Skywalker, what's up?" Pause. "No way, dude." From what I could tell, Walker was having some sort of gaming crisis. "Just go on the attack. If Doomringer's a noob, he'll try to hide behind the temple wall." While Tyler launched a series of directions, his eyes darting wildly as if watching the action live, Jax pulled me aside.

"I'm kinda nervous about meeting her," she said.

"Me, too." A funny feeling had settled in my stomach. Maybe it was the pizza-flavored chips I'd eaten during the ride, combined with the mini doughnuts, but it felt like more than that. I was jittery, on the verge of turning around and heading back to the car. What if Juniper was living off the radar because she was some kind of crazy person?

"Let's go," Jax said, then she hurried across the street.

Tyler, who was still commanding the attack on Doomringer, seemed totally uninterested in the real world at the moment. "Flank him!" he yelled into the phone. "Listen to me. You can't take down the temple without more life points. You have to kill Doomringer first. Use the Sword of Athena. And watch out for the Gorgons!"

I rolled my eyes. My parents worry about *me*?

Jax had already reached the door and was knocking. There wasn't much movement around the row houses. A man at the far end was mowing his little strip of grass. A few cars passed by. Tyler slashed the air with an imaginary sword as he continued to direct the assault. A jogger slowed and gawked at him.

I joined Jax on the porch. As I tried to steady my breathing, she knocked again.

"No one's home," I said, totally relieved. "We can still get to DC and check into our hotel before Mom gets off work and calls to check on us."

"Why are you so quick to give up?" Jax asked.

"I'm not leaving until I find out about the box."

"But if she's not here, we can't ask her about the box."

"I have a feeling and I'm not leaving."

"What kind of feeling?"

"Some feelings can't be explained. Besides, we came all this way." This time she pounded on the door. It rattled, then creaked open about an inch. We both stepped back. "It wasn't locked," she whispered.

"Why wouldn't she lock the door?" I whispered back. "Everybody locks the front door."

Jax leaned close to the crack. "Hello?" she called. No one answered. "Hello?"

"Uh . . . doesn't it seem weird that someone who would lock a box with a secret code wouldn't lock her own front door?"

"Yeah, that does seem weird." We kept whispering. "Maybe she forgot. I think we should go in."

"That's trespassing," I pointed out. "Trespassing is against the law."

Jax narrowed her eyes. "Only if there's a sign that says *No Trespassing*. And I don't see a sign so it's not against the law."

Her logic was flawed. "No one puts up a sign that

says *No Stealing* or *No Murdering* but it's still against the law."

"Ethan, you're worrying about nothing." Jax beamed a confident smile. "It's not trespassing because the door was open *and* because we're family."

"But . . ." This place did not give off a friendly vibe. There was no welcome mat. The curtains were shut tight. At least the house next door had a little gnome statue out front. "What if it's a fake address, like Tyler suggested, and someone else lives here? Someone who might freak out if we go inside without being invited?"

"Hmmmm." She pursed her lips. "Just in case . . . don't leave any fingerprints." Using her elbow, she gently pushed the door open. Then she stepped inside.

I looked back across the street. Tyler was still caught up in his phone call, hacking his way through the Gorgons or beheading a Cyclops, I couldn't be sure. I waved at him, hoping he'd notice his brother and cousin as we disappeared into a strange woman's house, uninvited. But his back was to us. The jogger was gone and the guy on the lawn mower had driven around to the other side, out of view. I took a deep breath and followed Jax. Trespassing was trespassing, no matter how she tried to spin it.

Light streamed in through the front door. The living room was a disaster. "Now we know where Tyler gets his slob gene," Jax said as she stood, hands on hips, scanning the mess.

But not even Tyler was this much of a slob. Furniture lay upturned, drawers were open, a lamp lay shattered. "It looks like someone broke in."

"That would explain the unlocked door," Jax said. Then she lowered her voice and grabbed my arm. "Do you think they're still here?"

My heart skipped a beat.

We stood frozen, listening. The lawn mower hummed in the distance but no sounds came from within the house. I opened my phone, prepared to dial 911 just in case. Jax grabbed a poker from the fireplace. "What are you doing?" I whispered.

"Come on, let's search the rooms."

Against my better judgment, which was nothing new these days, I followed her into the only bedroom. The bed had been taken apart, the dresser drawers overturned. There were a few pieces of clothes on the carpet, a pair of shoes, and a plain black suitcase. The bathroom had also been searched, but the only toiletries were a toothbrush, toothpaste, and some shampoo. Then, we found the office.

This room was crammed with personal stuff, like photos and knickknacks. Papers and files lay all over the place, as if a mini twister had hit. After setting the poker aside, Jax reached for a broken picture frame. "I thought you were worried about fingerprints," I said, handing her a clean tissue from my pocket.

"Oh, right. Thanks." Using the tissue, she picked up the frame. "Hey, I think this is me. I recognize the hat." Behind a sheet of broken glass, the frame held a photo of a woman and a baby. The baby wore a knit cap with a daisy on the front. The woman was middle-aged, with straw-colored hair that hung in two long braids. She was smiling at the baby. Scrawled in black pen along the bottom of the photo were the words *Jax and Me*. "Do you think that's Juniper?"

"Maybe. She looks a bit like your mom," I realized. Then I froze.

Jax gasped. She dropped the frame and grabbed the fireplace poker. We both whipped around and faced the office door.

Someone was walking through the house.

14
JAX

I gripped the fireplace poker in both hands, aiming it at the doorway. The robber had returned, or maybe he'd never left. Maybe he'd been hiding in the closet and as soon as he figured out we were kids, he decided to deal with us.

Ethan was probably thinking the same thing because he grabbed a book and held it like he was going to throw it. Then he must have decided that a book made a terrible weapon, because he pulled his Swiss army knife from his pocket. As the footsteps closed in, we huddled side by side like two raccoons caught in headlights. Someone appeared in the doorway. I lunged.

"Hey! What's your problem?" Tyler cried, ducking as I swung. "You almost poked out my eye. Are you trying to turn me into a Cyclops?"

My arms fell to my sides. "Don't do that," I said between clenched teeth.

"Do what?"

"Sneak up on us. I almost peed my pants." I set the poker on the desk. Ethan stood frozen, the knife still clenched in his hands.

"Are you going to stab me with that toothpick?" Tyler asked him, arching one of his eyebrows. I'd tried to teach myself how to raise one eyebrow, practicing in the mirror until my forehead had started to throb. Tyler looked devilish when he did it. When I tried, it always looked like I was holding back a fart.

"Don't tempt me," Ethan said, then he put the knife away.

"So what's going on?" Tyler asked. "Why's everything on the floor?"

"Someone broke in and robbed the place," I told him. "Either that or our great-aunt is a slob. She's not here so we can't ask."

"If she's not here, how'd you get in?"

"The door was unlocked." My attention was

drawn back to the photo labeled *Jax and Me*. Tyler was the only one of us old enough to remember our great-aunt so he might recognize her. "Is this Juniper?" I asked.

He picked up the photo. "Yeah, I think so. I remember those long braids."

I took in more details. Juniper was holding me and smiling into the camera. Her face was tan and weathered from the sun. She had a big, broad smile and a gap in her front teeth. A bright red bandana wound around her neck. "The building behind us looks old," I said, pointing to a white building with columns. "Do you think this photo was taken in Greece?"

"That's the Lincoln Memorial," Ethan said.

"How do you know?" I asked.

"Don't you remember? Two years ago, when my nosebleeds got bad, Dad took me to DC to see a specialist. We had some extra time so we visited the memorial." Then he pulled a five-dollar bill out of his wallet. "You might recognize the memorial because it's on our money. See?"

"The Lincoln Memorial is in Washington, DC?" I asked. Ethan nodded. "You know, last night, Mom told me that I'd visited DC when I was a baby. This photo must have been taken during that trip." I searched the photo for clues. A group of tourists stood at the memorial's entrance, old-fashioned cameras hanging around their necks. Mom wasn't in the picture so maybe she'd been the one taking it. "This must have been before the family got mad at Juniper."

"Here's another photo," Ethan said, picking a black frame off a pile of papers. A younger Juniper stood in some kind of ruin, surrounded by crumbling stone walls and broken pillars. She wore her hair in the same long braids. She was dressed in a khaki shirt and shorts, with a blue bandana around her neck.

"She looks like an extra in that movie *Raiders of the Lost Ark*," Tyler said.

"Hey, here's a diploma." Ethan pointed to a frame that hung lopsided on the wall. "Master of science in archaeology."

"She's an archaeologist?" I smiled, imagining all the exciting things my great-aunt must have done in her life, like finding a Pharaoh's tomb or digging up a pirate treasure or discovering a lost city near the Amazon. "Wow. I bet she's been all over the world."

"From the American University in Athens, awarded to Juniper Jacqueline Vandegrift," he read.

Did I hear correctly? "Hey, wait. I'm named after her?" Not only had we taken a trip to DC with her, but my mother had named me in her honor. This was clear evidence that Juniper had once been loved by my family. Why had that changed?

For the next fifteen minutes or so, we went through the office, looking at photos and documents. There were pictures of Juniper at excavation sites, wielding a shovel and pick, holding fragments of pottery. Sometimes she was in a group, sometimes alone. Locations were scrawled along the bottom of the photos. *The Palace of Knossos on Crete. The Agora in Athens. The Temple of Zeus on Mt. Lykaion.*

I realized that I'd broken my fingerprint rule. So had Ethan. And Tyler, with his rapid-fire gaming fingers, was touching stuff, too. Maybe it didn't matter, now that we knew for sure that this was our great-aunt's house. But there was still a possibility that the place had been robbed and the police would want to dust for prints. I was about to ask

Ethan for more tissues, when a newspaper clipping caught my eye.

Mysterious Illness at Excavation Site, the headline read. The article's black-and-white photo showed a man lying on a stretcher. "Hey, listen to this." I read it out loud:

A mysterious illness hit workers at an excavation site on the island of Kassos. The twelve-member team reported no unusual symptoms until Monday morning when, at the same moment, everyone was suddenly struck with overwhelming fatigue and dark thoughts. One person was not affected, however, and radioed for medical help. All team members were flown to Athens, where doctors were baffled. "We cannot explain the symptoms," Dr. Farouk, head of exotic diseases, said. "They are awake but seem uninterested in conversation or food, as if they've retreated into their own minds. The prognosis is uncertain." The unaffected team member, a woman who refused to give her name, disappeared before being interviewed.

The excavation was funded by an anonymous company but no further information was available.

"Weird," I said, staring at the man on the stretcher. His eyes were wide open, his face expressionless. He looked like he was under some sort of spell. The whole thing struck me as creepy.

Ethan held up another photo. "Look at this." I peered over his shoulder. A man and a woman stood on either side of Juniper. The man had a thin mustache and a beak-like nose. He held a shovel. The woman had ebony skin and was very tall. She also held a shovel. Like Juniper, they were dressed in safari-type clothing. A shiver ran up my spine.

"The Hatmakers," Ethan and I said at the same time.

Tyler, who'd been looking at some kind of fossil, did a double take. "Hatmakers? Are you talking about the people who broke my car window? Let me see that." He snatched the photo from Ethan's hands. "I thought you said they were old."

"They *are* old," Ethan said. "That photo must have been taken a long time ago."

"Camels in the desert," Tyler said, reading the handwriting along the bottom of the photo. "Camels in the desert? I don't get it. There aren't any camels in this photo."

It wasn't the missing camels that surprised me.

What I noticed was that the Hatmakers each had an arm wrapped around Juniper's waist, as if they were . . . "It looks like they're friends," I said. "The Hatmakers and Juniper are friends. Look how happy they are." They were smiling as if they'd won the lottery.

I sat in the desk chair, trying to piece together the facts. "Juniper and the Hatmakers know each other. It looks like they worked together. And the Hatmakers stole the puzzle box, which was sent to me by Juniper." The pieces began to fall into place. A black Jaguar had pulled up alongside us shortly after leaving Chatham, New Jersey. "They weren't out for a nice drive and just happened to run into us at the gas station. They followed us. They wanted the box."

"You think the Hatmakers came here looking for the box?" Ethan asked. "You think they're the ones who made this mess?"

"It makes sense," I said, slowly nodding.

"So if they came here, but didn't find the box, how did they figure out you had it?"

"This," Tyler said. He picked up a UPS delivery receipt that clearly showed my address. The date of delivery was my birthday.

"Uh . . . let me get this straight." Ethan sat on the edge of the desk. "They ransacked Juniper's house, followed us to the gas station, and broke Tyler's window, just so they could get that metal box." He paused. "That must mean—"

"That there *is* something inside." I leaped to my feet, excitement dancing down my legs. "Don't you see, this is proof that the box holds something amazing. The Hatmakers are archaeologists, just like Juniper. She must have found something and whatever it is, they want it. They want it *bad*." I couldn't believe this was happening. Finally, an adventure for Jax Malone. "This is like a movie."

"Well, it's not a movie," Ethan pointed out. "The Hatmakers are real. And we should call the police and turn them in." He was being his usual self. Oh why couldn't he just get caught up in the excitement of the moment? Why did he always have to be so cautious?

"What do you think is inside my box?" I wondered dreamily.

Tyler picked up a glass paperweight and held it up to the window. As he spun it, mini rainbows reflected onto the walls. "In Space Quest X, deep inside the volcanic cave of the Moon of Serenity, lies the Box of Banishment. And inside the box is a wormhole that leads into another dimension. There are players who would literally kill to get that box. Only two have managed—a guy from Korea and a kid from New Zealand."

"The Box of Banishment?" Ethan groaned. "Tyler, this isn't Space Quest X. This is the *real* world."

"I know this is the *real* world. I'm not confused about which dimension I'm currently inhabiting. Jeez." Tyler rolled his eyes. "I'm just saying that there are lots of quests where a box holds an amazing prize. The Ark of the Covenant, for example. The ark was basically a really large golden box that contained the stone tablets with the Ten Commandments. Of course there's Pandora's box, which contained evil, and then there are all the pirate stories about treasure chests—those are boxes too. And . . ." He set the paperweight back on the desk. "But that doesn't matter because our box is long gone. And no box means no prize. Quest terminated. I'm gonna go home and work with Walker on the game." He headed out the office door, car keys dangling from his fingers. "But first, I'm thirsty."

Go home? "Wait, Tyler," I called as Ethan and I followed.

"We should at least call the police," Ethan said.

"This entire day has been a colossal waste." Tyler headed into the kitchen. "A black hole of time suck, that's what it's been." He grabbed a cup off a shelf, then filled it at the sink. Like the other rooms, the kitchen had been searched. The cupboard drawers and oven had been left open. Silverware lay scattered.

"But we can still find my . . . I mean, *our* box," I insisted. I wished I'd never agreed to share it with Tyler, but a deal was a deal. And I still needed his help, *and* his car. "Come on. Don't give up. Think about the quest for that other box you mentioned . . . the Ark of the Cover."

"Ark of the Covenant," Tyler corrected. "Jeez."

"Yeah, that thing." I'd never read the story so I didn't have the slightest clue what I was talking about. But I refused to let this adventure come to a big disappointing ending! Using my best persuasive voice, and trying not to fidget too much, I said, "They wanted the Ark and so they went and got it, right? They did whatever it took. They didn't give up."

"Well, they should have," Tyler said. "Because they ended up being visited by a plague of rats, boils, and hemorrhoids."

Rats, boils, and hemorrhoids? Who wrote a weird story like that?

As Tyler gulped with all the delicacy of a wild boar, Ethan stood quietly in the corner. He had his phone in hand, waiting for someone to say it was okay to call the police. "Tyler," I pleaded. "Please don't go home yet. If we find Juniper, then she'll tell us the right spot where the box opens. And then we can go to the right spot, find the Hatmakers, and get the box back." It wasn't a ridiculous plan. It made total sense. Didn't it?

"Uh, guys," Ethan said as he pointed to the kitchen floor. "Is that what I think it is?"

I looked down. My stomach went queasy. A red splotch lay on the floor.

"Is that . . . ?" I cringed. "Is that *blood*?"

15
JAX

It didn't matter if it was or wasn't blood, just the thought made my stomach churn. It was embarrassing, really. Why did I always react that way? I was brave about most everything else.

The splotch was the size of a quarter. Another lay about a foot away. A third splotch was spread thin by a shoe's imprint.

Tyler put the cup in the sink, then crouched next to the first splotch. "It looks like ketchup," he said.

I didn't want to get close to it. "How do we tell?" I asked.

"Well, blood has a metallic taste and ketchup is sweet," he said.

"Taste?" I felt a gag coming on.

Ethan gasped. "Are you insane? You can't taste someone else's blood. Blood carries pathogens."

"I wasn't going to taste it," Tyler said. "I'm not batcrap crazy. I was going to get one of you to taste it." He opened the refrigerator. "FYI, there's no ketchup in here."

My heart thudded. Blood on the floor and no great-aunt to be found. "How long do you think it's been here?" I asked.

"It's dry, so it's not fresh," Ethan said. "Dad would be able to do an analysis."

"Do *not* call your dad," I said. Sure, Uncle Phil had his own laboratory and all sorts of equipment, but calling him would be just as bad as calling my mom. Our "quest" would be over.

Then a horrid thought crept into my mind. "If the Hatmakers broke in and were searching the place, and if Juniper interrupted them, or tried to stop them . . ." I swallowed hard. "Do you think they hurt her?"

We stood in silence for a moment. Then Tyler launched into a wild explanation. "What if the Hatmakers sneaked up on Juniper and whacked her on the head, just like in the movies? Then Juniper crumpled to the floor like a rag doll. The drops of blood trickled from her temple as they dragged her away."

"Uh . . ." Ethan's voice cracked. "Now I'm definitely calling the police."

"Wait," I said. "We don't know for sure that she's hurt. Let's just see if we can figure out what happened." Ethan frowned, then put his phone away. I looked around the kitchen. An open loaf of bread sat on the counter, along with a block of cheddar cheese. "What if she was about to make a sandwich and she cut herself?" The footprint pointed toward the back kitchen door. "Then she walked outside because she needed to get a bandage at the drugstore. Or she needed to go to the clinic to get stitches. That would explain the drops and the footprint."

Tyler stood next to the print. "Well, your hypothesis works if our great-aunt is some kind of behemoth. I wear a size twelve and this print is bigger."

She didn't look like a behemoth in the photos. In fact, she was short compared to both Hatmakers.

Stepping carefully over the print, I peered out the kitchen door. Parking spots lined the alleyway behind the row houses. A blue car was parked right outside. "Where are you going?" Ethan asked as I turned the knob.

"I want to see if that's Juniper's car."

It was a little two-door car, a hybrid. A bill from the power company sat on the front seat, addressed to Occupant. A safari hat sat on the backseat, along with a green bandana. Like me with my purple coat, Juniper seemed to have a signature look. "It's her car," I announced as I hurried back into the kitchen. "So where is she?"

"Maybe she went for a walk," Ethan said.

"Why would she go for a walk if she's dripping blood?" Tyler reached his hand into the bread bag and pulled out two slices. "That seems stupid." He shoved them into his mouth.

A new idea took shape. "What if the blood doesn't belong to Juniper?" I said. "If the Hatmakers made this mess, then maybe one of them got cut during the rampage and Mr. Hatmaker left that footprint on his way out."

"Or . . ." Tyler swallowed. "Maybe they didn't knock her over the head. Maybe they stabbed her and carried her dead body out the back door."

"Dead body?" Ethan said.

"Yeah." He reached for more bread. "And then they dumped the body in the river."

Ethan pulled out his phone real quick, like a Wild West sheriff drawing a gun. Before he could dial, I yanked it from his hand. "Just wait," I said. The last thing we needed was for Ethan to freak out and call the police. I'd promised Mom no trouble. Okay, so maybe I was more worried about myself than about Ethan and Tyler, but they hadn't been caught shoplifting a candy bar, so their parents weren't prepared to ground them for life if they made one more mistake. I glared at Tyler. "You are *not* helping. Ethan and I are trying to come up with *real* scenarios. We have no proof that she's been stabbed or that she's dead."

"We have no proof she's alive, either," Tyler retorted, then he bit off a chunk of cheese.

My stomach growled but I ignored it. "Look," I said, "we don't even know if she's missing. She erased herself from the internet, remember? She doesn't want to be found. Let's ask around and see if the neighbors know anything."

So we knocked on some of the row-house doors. A woman with a big birthmark on her face answered. She didn't know Juniper personally but she'd seen her. Juniper had lived there for a few weeks but they'd never spoken. The man who'd been mowing the lawn said he'd seen the old lady who lived in the last house but he didn't know her name. She always kept her curtains closed. "She's real private," he told us. Ethan called the local hospital but no one named Juniper Vandegrift had been admitted.

After much begging and pleading on my part, I convinced Tyler to give me a bit more time before we headed home. Also, I promised him another Starbucks card even though I had no idea how I was going to pay for it. So we went back to Juniper's office to see if we could find more clues. I picked up the photo of the Hatmakers with their arms around Juniper, big smiles on their faces. *The Camels in the desert.* Something about it was bugging me. Why give a photo a label about camels if there are no camels? "The Camels in the desert. The Camels in the desert. Wait a minute. *Camels* is capitalized!" That changed everything. I found an address book peeking out from beneath a pile of papers.

"You think that's their name?" Ethan asked.

"It could be," I said as I flipped through the

pages. "Now that I think about it, Hatmaker sounds totally fake. Hello? Here it is! Martha and George Camel. Remember? He called her Martha. Oh but wait, there are two addresses. The first is in Greece, the second is in London. No phone numbers for either one."

"Martha and George Camel," Ethan said. He searched on his phone. "Uh . . . they have a bunch of hits. They're listed as members of the International Society of Archaeologists and they graduated from the American University in Athens, same as Juniper. There are some articles that George wrote about Greek history. The British Museum gave him some sort of award." Ethan's fingers danced across the screen, jumping from site to site. His fingers stopped. "Listen to this. According to another article, the Camels were involved in a mysterious incident at an archaeological site where they were both struck by an unknown illness."

"Struck by an unknown illness?" I grabbed the newspaper article and looked at the photo of the man on the stretcher. It was difficult to tell, but there was a slight resemblance to the old man who'd tried to buy my box at the fruit stand. He had the same long nose.

"Martha Camel owned an auction house in London where she specialized in ancient artifacts," Ethan said, still searching on his phone. "There's an article in the *London Times*. The auction house closed after a scandal. Looks like she sold something she wasn't supposed to sell. They disappeared and haven't been seen since."

"Until they busted my car window," Tyler said as he shoved another piece of bread into his mouth.

I searched through the address book again and found a sticky note inside the front cover. Written in the handwriting I was starting to recognize were the initials M. & G. C., followed by an address for the Sunny Days Motel. "M. and G. C.—Martha and George Camel!" I handed the note to Ethan. "Where is this place?"

"Not far," he said. "We passed it on the way into town." Then he frowned. "Uh, no way. We're not going after them." He took off his baseball cap and wiped a bit of sweat from his forehead. "Are we?"

My mind was racing so fast, I had to grab my thoughts and line them up, one by one. My feet wanted to race too, straight out of the row house and back to Tyler's car so we could begin the pursuit! "Look," I said. "If we want to get the box, which we do, we have to find these people. And since we don't know the right spot, the only other choice is to go to their house."

"Actually, there are other choices," Ethan said as he stuck his hat on. "We could go home. Or we could go to the hotel like we're supposed to."

"I don't like those choices," I said. I felt desperate for anything that might convince Ethan to not give up. Our great-aunt wasn't here. She couldn't help us. But the box was with the Camels and I wanted it back. "Just remember this one thing—the Camels were willing to pay a lot of money for that box. And they broke laws to get it. It's got something valuable inside. So valuable that you have to solve a puzzle just to see it."

Ethan was still holding the sticky note with the Camels' address. He looked at it. Was he considering? Then he shook his head. "No way. I promised Mom that I wouldn't let you get me into trouble. I say we call the police and—"

Tyler snatched the sticky note. Then he held it high above his head, as if holding a torch. "No puzzle shall remain unsolved. I hereby declare that the quest has been rebooted. Objective—to disable the Camels and retrieve the secret box. Onward, minions." He turned on his heels and headed out the office door.

"Yay!" I cheered. Then I patted Ethan's shoulder. "I couldn't do this without you, partner."

Ethan sighed. "That box is the worst birthday present ever."

16
ETHAN

FACT: *Sidekicks were invented so the superhero had a loyal assistant. Sherlock Holmes had Dr. Watson, the Lone Ranger had Tonto, Frodo had Samwise. The sidekick is supposed to perform functions that the hero can't perform. Dr. Watson helped solve crimes, Tonto helped bring justice to the Wild West, and Samwise killed a giant spider and became a ring bearer. What did I do?*

I looked things up on my phone.

"Did you get the directions?" Jax asked.

"Yeah."

I hadn't realized it before, but Tyler and Jax had one big thing in common—they were stubborn. When they wanted something, there was no giving in. Jax sat in the front seat, humming along to the battle march of the orcs or trolls or whatever mythological monster inhabited the soundtrack. Tyler thumped his hand on the steering wheel. They were a team. I would have never imagined Jax and Tyler working together. Until today, she couldn't stand him. And now they were like Bonnie and Clyde, those gangsters who robbed banks. Jax and Tyler, united on their quest for the box. What they didn't seem to understand was that not everything had to be a conquest of some sort.

Or maybe that's where I had it wrong. Maybe that's why Tyler had shelves of trophies and I didn't.

I checked the time. Mom would be calling soon. What would I tell her?

"Hey, Ethan, can you read that article?" Jax asked.

"What article?"

"The one you found online. The one about the Camels getting into some kind of trouble." She turned off the music.

I found the article and read it out loud.

ARCHAEOLOGISTS WANTED FOR FRAUD

The International Society of Archaeologists released an official statement today. Two of its members, George and Martha Camel, owners of Camel Auction House in London, have been ejected from the respected institution after evidence of forgery and fraud surfaced. The society collected proof that the pair advertised and sold ancient artifacts, most of which were fake. Attention was drawn to the auction house when the Camels announced that they were in possession of the famous Pandora's box. An auction for the box was held privately, with an unnamed source paying an undisclosed amount of money. The box was not delivered to the buyer and the Camels have since disappeared.

"Pandora's box?" Jax said. "Hey, Tyler, you mentioned that earlier. What is it?"

"It's a box that contains evil," he said. "Walker and I've been working on a design for Pandora's box in Cyclopsville. Once you get into the temple and pry open the vault, you take Pandora's box to the Cyclops king and he rewards you with entrance to the next level. But if you open it before giving it to the Cyclops King, then your head explodes and the rest of your body bursts into flame. It's awesome."

"So if you've put it into your game, does that mean it's a Greek myth?" she asked.

"Yeah, it's a Greek myth." He snorted. "Once again, the public education system has failed to enlighten the masses. Unbelievable."

I'd heard of Pandora's box, but I didn't know the story either. "Tyler, could you give us a break from the insults and just tell us what you're talking about? But first take a right at this intersection." I'd switched back to Google Maps. "Uh . . . right. Go right!"

The wheels squealed as Tyler made a sharp turn. The plastic-wrap window was holding nicely in place.

"Why's it called Pandora's box?" Jax asked.

"According to Greek mythology, Pandora was the first woman on earth."

"You mean like Eve?" Jax asked.

"Yeah, just like Eve. Pandora was the Greek Eve. Before she arrived, there were only men on earth. Zeus, the leader of the gods, was mad at men for some reason, I can't remember."

I almost snorted. Tyler had just admitted to not knowing something. That was like a mini miracle.

"Anyway, Zeus was angry with men so he invented women as revenge."

"That's not very nice," Jax snapped.

"Don't get cranky with me. I didn't write the story." Tyler scratched his armpit. "Because Pandora was the first woman, and it was her birthday, the gods gave her all sorts of gifts like speech and beauty and clothing. Zeus gave her a box but he told her that she wasn't supposed to open it."

Jax sat up real straight. "Pandora got a box for her birthday? Just like me?"

"That's right, Sherlock. A box. Unfortunately, one of the other gifts was curiosity, so of course, being curious, she opened the box. Turns out it contained evil."

"Take a left," I said, checking the directions. "Uh . . . left. Left!"

Tires screeched again.

"What kind of evil?" Jax asked.

"What do you mean what kind of evil? Evil is evil. It's the opposite of good." Tyler turned the wheel. "The point is, when Pandora opened the box, evil escaped and was spread throughout the world. And that's why humanity is in such a mess all the time. That's why we're doomed."

Jax scowled. "That's stupid. Why are women always to blame in these old stories? Eve ate the apple and mankind was doomed with sin. Pandora opened the box and mankind was doomed with evil. It's totally unfair." She had a point.

"Speaking of apples, give me one, will ya?" Tyler held out his hand. I took three apples out of the fruit-stand bag and we all munched.

"I don't understand something," I said. "Pandora's box is a story. But the Camels claimed that they had it and they put it up for auction. And someone tried to buy it. Why would someone buy a box that doesn't exist?"

"A good con artist can talk anyone into buying anything," Tyler said.

I scooted low in my seat. Great. Not only were the Camels thieves who'd ransacked a house and broken our car window, they were also con artists. This was getting better by the minute.

"You don't think . . ." Jax turned and stared at me over the seat. "What if it's not just a story? What if the box Juniper sent to me is Pandora's box?"

Tyler tapped his fingers on the steering wheel. "Not likely. They didn't have GPS technology in ancient Greece. That box is twenty-first-century design."

"Yeah, I guess you're right." She turned back around. "I'm glad it's not a box full of evil. That would be a total drag."

"Unless you wanted to take over the world."

I sighed. They were both mental.

Ten minutes later, we reached our destination. This place that was the exact opposite of New Hope. No crafts shops, no art galleries or overflowing flowerpots. The road was lined with fast-food joints, gas stations, and a couple of motels, the kind that offered weekly and monthly room rentals. Google Maps led us to one of these motels, two stories tall, brick, with powder-blue trim on the windows. The sign advertised kitchenettes and microwave ovens in every room. A row of garbage cans cluttered the sidewalk. It looked like someone had driven a truck into the side of each one. An old broken television lay next to the cans, along with a broken broom and a battered motorcycle helmet.

"What a dump," Tyler said.

"Look for their car," Jax said.

We drove around the building twice, but didn't see a black Jaguar, which made me feel a bit better. As much as I wanted Jax to have her birthday present, it would be nice to avoid a big scene. Tyler passed two perfectly good parallel-parking spots, claiming he was "surveying the terrain." Then he parked at the far side of the building.

"What's the plan?" I asked before we got out.

"To get the box," Jax said.

"Great," I mumbled. "No plan."

A couple of kids were swinging on a rusty swing set at the edge of the parking lot. A woman sat on a bench nearby, reading a magazine. The day was warm, so many of the motel windows were open, with music and television soundtracks leaking out. Wet laundry lay on windowsills to dry. This was no vacation spot. People were living here—people who were down and out on their luck.

"Room Two C," Tyler said as he read the sticky note he'd taken from Juniper's office.

The Sunny Days Motel was designed so that all the doors faced the road. Jax took the lead, marching up the steps with determination. We walked along the balcony until we came to room 2C. Traffic whizzed by, which made me feel a bit better. The Camels wouldn't try to hurt us, not with so many witnesses around. I reminded myself that they were old people, and that we could easily overpower them. Jax was good at wrestling and Tyler was six foot two. I felt around in my pocket until my fingers rested on the Swiss army knife. Just in case.

The door had a peephole. Jax covered it with her hand. Down the balcony, a TV blared, pots and pans clinked. It smelled like someone was making grilled cheese. My stomach growled super loud. Both Tyler and Jax shot me a glare. I glared right back. How was I supposed to keep my stomach from growling? I hadn't eaten anything all day except those mini doughnuts, the pizza-flavored chips, and a couple of apples.

Jax pressed her ear to the door. Then she knocked. And knocked again.

"They're not here," I said with relief. "Let's go."

"Looks like a dead end," Tyler whispered.

"There's no such thing as a dead end," Jax said, knocking louder and louder.

"Actually there is," Tyler corrected. "We built one in Cyclopsville."

"This is *not* a dead end," she insisted, grabbing the knob and wiggling it. She wiggled it again and again, then pushed her shoulder against the door.

"Uh . . . what are you doing?" I asked, looking

around to make sure we hadn't drawn attention. "It's locked. Jax, stop it."

But she didn't stop. With a grunt she pushed harder and harder, her face turning red. Then she grabbed the knob with both hands. "The box is inside this room," she said, her teeth clenched. "I know it's in there." Strands of hair fell out of her ponytail and dangled in her eyes. Her knuckles turned white.

"She's going berserk," Tyler said in a matter-of-fact way.

She was. She was about to throw her entire body against the door but I squeezed in front of her. "Jax," I said, my voice low and calm, as if talking to a rabid dog. "Why would the box be inside if the Camels aren't here?"

She took a long breath, then unclenched her hands. "I have a feeling. And I've never had a feeling like this before."

"A feeling?" Tyler asked.

"It's in there. Trust me." She undid her ponytail and remade it, tighter and neater. Oh no. She wasn't giving up. "I'm getting my box."

"Wait a minute." I kept my voice low. "Maybe we didn't *technically* break into Juniper's house because the door was unlocked and we're family, but there's no way we can go into the Camels' motel room unless we're invited. Otherwise, it's definitely trespassing."

She ignored me, which is what she did when I didn't agree with her. And she marched back down the stairs and over to the woman who sat reading the magazine. Tyler and I followed, except I stood back a ways, watching. It always amazed me that Jax could walk up to anyone and start talking. "Excuse me," she said. The woman looked up, her lip curled. Jax had interrupted her reading. I could relate. "I'm looking for my grandparents. He's bald and walks with a cane. And she's really tall and has silver hair."

"I don't know 'em," the woman said. She turned the page. It was one of those magazines that was all about celebrities. The movie star on the cover had been labeled the worst dressed.

"Is there an office manager, or someone who might have an extra key to my grandparents' room?" Jax asked.

"The manager's only here in the morning. Then he goes and gets drunk. He won't be no help to you." She turned and hollered at her kid. "Max, stop throwing sand on your brother!"

A couple of teens, dressed in ripped jeans and high-tops, walked past. With Jax in the lead, we followed them into the motel laundry room. An old tan dryer bounced from side to side, overloaded. Cigarette butts had been swept into the corner. Junk mail was piled on a counter, next to empty boxes of Tide.

"Hey," Jax said. "I'm looking for my grandparents." She described them.

The girl wore a gold chain that connected her nose piercing to her ear piercing. When she shook her head, the chain swayed. I wondered about the intelligence behind attaching two parts of your face that weren't supposed to be attached. If she got that chain caught on something, she'd rip an earlobe *and* a nostril. "What's your problem?" she asked me with a sneer. "What are you staring at?"

"Uh . . . nothing," I murmured, stepping back.

"Maybe you'll remember their car," Tyler said. "They drive a black jag."

The guy, who'd been texting, quickly glanced at Tyler. "Yeah, I know that car. I helped the old man carry in some suitcases."

"When?"

"I don't know. Few days ago." He kept texting.

"They paid me one hundred bucks. Cash."

"One hundred bucks to carry suitcases?" Tyler whistled. "That's good money. If they can pay that, then they can pay for my car window for sure."

"We came to see them but they're not here and the office manager isn't here either," Jax told the guy. "Do you know if there's anyone else who might have an extra key?"

He texted something, then said, "We always climb in through the windows when we lock ourselves out. They open super easy. Just slide a knife under the frame. Everyone does it. There's a ladder out back."

"Really? Thanks," Jax said, then she started around the building without a word. Uh, shouldn't breaking into a motel be a group decision? Whatever happened to democracy?

"We're going to end up in the back of a police car," I grumbled.

An alley ran between the motel and some sort of warehouse. There were no doors back there, but each of the rooms had two windows that offered a boring view of the warehouse's cement wall. Jax counted along the second floor, then pointed. "That's Two C." Curtains were drawn, the windows closed tight. A ladder lay on the ground. "We're not really going to do this," I said. But Jax had already grabbed it.

A memory flashed across my mind. When we were little, Jax spotted a bird nest in the tree outside her bedroom. She waited weeks for the baby birds to leave the nest, then she tried to climb the tree. When that didn't work, she got a ladder. When that didn't work, she got a table. I was opposed to setting the ladder on the table but she talked me into it. A minute later she was lying on the grass, cradling a broken elbow. The paramedics were nice. One of them climbed the ladder and scooped the nest right up. But we both got grounded.

Watching her grab that ladder, I got the same feeling of foreboding as when we were little. "Uh, Jax, I don't think—"

"It'll be okay."

Famous. Last. Words.

Two boys zipped into the alley on their bikes. As they rode past, Tyler and I froze, unsure what to do. But Jax smiled and waved. "We forgot our key," she told them. They didn't seem to care, just kept riding up and down. "If you act like you're not doing anything wrong, most people won't question you," Jax said. "Just look confident."

I'd heard that piece of wisdom countless times.

Turned out it was true. If you sit in the reserved section at the Chatham Playhouse, and you act as if you belong in the reserved section, no one asks any questions. But it still didn't feel right. Sometimes it felt like I was witnessing my life, watching myself from afar—there I was, up to my eyeballs in a Jax situation again.

As Tyler helped her lean the ladder against the wall, a woman on the first floor peered out at us. Jax smiled and waved at the woman. "We forgot our key."

"You need a knife?" the woman asked. "The kids above me use a knife to get in."

"We have a knife," Jax said, looking at me. I handed over my Swiss army knife. Then, trying to muster confidence, I smiled at the woman, but the smile felt forced and goofy.

A baby cried in the background. The woman closed the window and disappeared.

"You see, act like you belong and no one questions you," Jax said. "Hold the ladder, please."

Tyler, who'd been uncharacteristically quiet, shuffled in place. He shoved his hands into his pockets. "You know, I don't think this is trespassing. I think this is breaking and entering. If we get caught, this could really hurt my chances of getting into college."

Whoa! I almost passed out. The voice of reason had wormed its way into my brother. "Yes," I said, nodding my head like a bobble-headed doll. "Exactly. Breaking and entering will look really, really bad on your high-school transcript. It will look bad on all our transcripts. So let's not do this."

"What?" The word shot out of Jax's mouth. "You're going to back out now? But we're so close. How can you guys abandon . . . a *quest*?"

Tyler ran a hand over his tangled hair. "I'm hoping to get into Massachusetts Institute of Technology. If I get arrested, I won't even be able to get into Massachusetts Institute of Taxidermy." He stepped away from the ladder. I figured Tyler could get arrested for making meth in our basement and, because of his grades, he'd still get into the best college in the US. But I wasn't going to say that.

Jax sighed. "Fine. Whatever. I'll do it alone." She opened the Swiss army knife to its dull, flat blade. Then she began to climb the ladder. It rocked side to side so Tyler and I grabbed it and held it steady. We shared a look of powerlessness as she climbed.

"She's bossy," Tyler said.

"You have no idea," I grumbled.

The bike riders rode past again. I imagined them telling their parents about the bad kids who were breaking into the motel, then their parents calling the police. But they had a bag of cookies and, after propping their bikes against the warehouse wall, sat together and ate, watching us with curiosity. My nose tingled. Holding the ladder with one hand, I pulled a tissue from my pocket with the other hand and held it to my nostrils. Things were getting out of hand. Caution Boy needed to speak up. "Uh, Jax," I called.

She'd reached the second floor. Pressing her face against the window, she peered through the crack in the curtains. "I can't see much."

Tyler, distracted by the cookie bag, let go of the ladder. "Hey," he called to the kids. "Are those Nilla Wafers? I love those things."

I let the tissue float to the ground and grabbed the ladder with both hands. Luckily, the tingle had been a false alarm. "Jax!" I called again.

"The room looks empty," she announced. Then she shimmied the blade under the window and pushed it open. Leaning over the sill, she kept talking but I couldn't hear her anymore.

And then she fell in.

Or had she been pulled in?

"Jax?"

Tyler didn't even notice. He was paying the kids for the box of wafers. A long moment passed. Crud!

The ladder wobbled but I didn't care. I scrambled up.

17
JAX

I tried to break the fall with my hands but I hit the floor hard.

Holding my breath, my eyes darted left, then right. It looked like I was alone. Phew! Slowly, I got to my feet. My left knee felt bruised but other than that, I was okay.

Now to find the box.

Before, when I was standing outside the door of room 2C, I could practically feel the box. Its warmth against my fingers, its weight in my arms. It was like I was a moth being pulled toward light. I had to get inside and be reunited. It sounds crazy, I get that, but that's how it felt. And now that I was in the room, the sensation was stronger. Much, much stronger.

As far as motel rooms went, this one was not going to earn enough stars for any travel guides. The bedspread was thin and orange, the pillows flat and limp. The gold wallpaper looked like Christmas wrap, and the only painting in the room was a tacky seascape, the kind with neon blue waves and a fluorescent sunrise. A pair of suitcases sat in the corner, clothing spilling out. I recognized the church-lady dress that Mrs. Camel had worn at the gas station and the bow tie and suit Mr. Camel had worn. His cane lay on the bed.

"Are you okay?" Ethan asked. He'd climbed the ladder and was leaning over the windowsill.

Where was the box? It had to be here. I could sense it.

"Yeah, I'm fine." I began my search at the bedside table. A silver wig and a bald wig lay next to the lamp, along with a box labeled *Theatrical Makeup*. "Hey, look at this." I opened it and found a small white mustache and a tube of spirit gum for gluing the mustache into place. "They were in disguise," I told Ethan.

"They're wanted for fraud," he said. "Makes

sense that they'd wear disguises." He stayed on the ladder. "Jax, we need to get out of here. What if the Camels come back? Did you find the box?"

"No." I opened drawers, searching. Then I rifled through the bedding.

"Uh, Jax." Ethan climbed into the room. "Did you see this?"

Was it the box? I spun around. Ethan stood next to the television, staring at the wall. Seven symbols had been drawn on the wallpaper.

Πανδορα

That was really weird. Who draws on motel-room walls? A bunch of candles had been placed on the desk beneath the drawing, most burned down to stubs.

"Maybe the power went out," I said, looking under the bed. Then I went into the bathroom and searched beneath the sink and in the tub. "It wasn't in there," I announced.

"If the power went out, you'd put candles all over the room, to spread the light. You wouldn't put them all in one place." Ethan folded his arms, staring at the wall. "Do you think this looks like an altar? Like at church?" A few sooty trails marked the wallpaper where flames had licked too close. I tried to imagine the Camels crouched there, praying to some deity. An eerie shiver slithered up my spine.

"Do you think they belong to some sort of cult?" Ethan asked.

"You're giving me the creeps," I said. "Help me look for the box."

The feeling suddenly swelled and I turned toward the closet. It was in there, I was sure of it. But how could I know that?

My heart skipped a beat. A guy's voice rose in the distance and it didn't belong to Tyler. I couldn't tell what he was saying but the voice came closer and closer, then stopped outside the motel room door. A key jiggled in the lock.

Like plunging into ice water, panic gripped my entire body.

There was no time. Quick like a rabbit, Ethan shoved the ladder away from the sill, then closed the window. I'd never seen him move so fast. Just as the motel door opened, he grabbed my sleeve and with a yank I found myself in the bathroom. A sour stench of mildew rose as Ethan pushed the shower curtain aside. I almost fell as we scrambled into the tub. This was the worst place in the world to hide. We were totally trapped. They'd find us. Of course they'd find us. My heart pounded. I pressed against Ethan's back. For the first time in my life I found myself hiding behind my cousin. A disgusting piece of yellowing plastic was the only thing separating us from two criminal archaeologists who break car windows and steal birthday presents from twelve-year-old girls. Who might also have kidnapped a mysterious great-aunt and be members of some freaky cult.

The hotel door slammed shut. Both Ethan and I jumped at the sound.

Ethan closed the shower curtain and we held perfectly still, listening to the conversation.

"She's a stubborn woman." I recognized Mr. Camel's voice from the gas station. "She's always been stubborn."

"She'd better tell us how to open that box. If she doesn't . . ." That was Mrs. Camel. She sounded super angry. "I must know. I must!"

"Do not fret, my dear. She shall reveal her secrets. I simply need a bit more time to *coax* her."

"Coaxing isn't working," Mrs. Camel snapped.

"You're too soft. Juniper Vandegrift is an old fool and she won't tell us anything unless we use stronger methods. Do you hear me? Stronger methods!"

I swallowed hard. Juniper was alive. They had her and they were trying to get information from her. But did stronger methods mean they were going to torture her?

There were shuffling sounds as the Camels moved around the room. What were they doing? It was really smart of Ethan to have pushed the ladder and closed the window. But what if Tyler put the ladder back? Oh crud. Please don't put the ladder back.

"Thank the gods, the box is still here," Mrs. Camel said.

"Of course it's still here, darling. Who would look for a priceless artifact in a run-down motel safe?" Mr. Camel's voice was calm and soothing, the exact opposite of his wife's.

I knew it. The box was here. My feelings had been correct. I squeezed Ethan's arm.

"I refuse to play this stupid game of riddles," Mrs. Camel said. "We pushed the button. It said attempt eight of ten. If we push it again, it will say attempt nine of ten and we still won't understand

and then what will we have? One more push?" Her voice was strained. "I thought you were good at puzzles!"

"I never said I was good at puzzles," Mr. Camel replied. "I'm good at many other things, my dear, but not puzzles."

I clenched my jaw. How dare they push the button? My button. My box.

"But I want answers!"

Mr. Camel cleared his throat. "I'm doing my best. Patience is a virtue."

"Patience?" Something crashed to the floor. "Don't talk to me about patience. I've been waiting years. This is just like Juniper, to make things difficult. Oh how I despise her," Mrs. Camel hissed. "That box was clearly made by the Locksmith. We'll find him. We'll make him tell us how to open it!"

"Juniper doesn't know where the Locksmith is. No one knows. Juniper is the only person who can open that box. Perhaps we can blackmail her into telling us."

There was a slapping sound. "Stop being such an idiot!" Mrs. Camel cried. "Blackmail won't work. We need to scare her. We need to terrify her!"

Ethan shuddered. I pressed closer to him.

After a long pause, Mr. Camel spoke softly. "Juniper Vandegrift would rather die than give us the contents of the box. How can I terrify her if she's willing to die?"

Ethan's chest rose and fell in quiet, shallow breaths. My legs started to ache from standing so still. When Mrs. Camel finally spoke, her voice was full of wickedness. "Yes, you're right. She doesn't care about her own life. But would she care about someone else's life?"

"What do you mean?"

"Surely she wouldn't let someone else die. Someone she cared about. A member of her *family.*" She laughed evilly.

I narrowed my eyes. Wait. Was I hearing this correctly?

"That's an excellent idea, darling. Juniper clearly cares about the girl. And she trusted her enough to send her the box. So if we can get our hands on the girl and threaten to hurt her . . ."

I swallowed hard.

The girl was me.

18
JAX

I might have grabbed Ethan's arm to steady myself but I was worried that even the slightest movement of my sleeve through air would alert the Camels to our hiding spot. It felt as if I'd been punched in the stomach. My knees went weak. They were going to find me and hurt me if Juniper didn't tell them how to open the box.

A phone rang. Ethan inhaled sharply and reached into his pocket, his eyes wild. Neither of us had remembered to mute his phone! It rang again. Oh crud!

"Hello?" Mr. Camel said from the other room.

Ethan and I sighed with relief. It was Mr.

Camel's phone. As Ethan set his phone on silent mode, Mr. Camel spoke. "How did you get this number?" He must have pressed the speaker button so that Mrs. Camel could hear the conversation, because the sound of static filled the air, followed by a voice.

Are you trying to hide from me? It was a man's voice, thick with an accent.

"No, no, of course we aren't hiding from you," Mr. Camel said. "Why would we hide from you?" His voice quivered. I didn't blame him. The voice on the other end was icy and sounded like an evil villain from a movie. Only this wasn't a movie.

Where is it?

"We will deliver it you, just as we agreed. You can count on us."

If you double-cross me again, you will suffer the consequences.

"Double-cross you? Why would we double-cross you?" Mr. Camel laughed nervously. "We will deliver it as planned. You can trust us. You have our word."

Your word is the only thing keeping you alive.

The static stopped and the phone call ended.

Someone else wanted the box? This was getting

crazier and crazier. How many people knew about my birthday present? Ethan's phone lit up. A message from Tyler:

Hey doofus what R U doing?

Ethan texted back:

Camels R here. Hiding in bathroom.
Don't climb ladder!

More shuffling sounds came from the motel room as the Camels moved around. Were they packing?

Ethan's screen lit up again:

Why R Camels hiding in bathroom?

Ethan rolled his eyes. I might have laughed if I hadn't been one hundred percent ready to freak out.

Do not climb ladder!!!

"I will never give him the box," Mrs. Camel said. "It's mine. Do you understand? Mine!"

Wow, I recognized that sound in her voice. She wanted the box as much as I did. Except for one thing—it belonged to me. It was my birthday present. She stole it. I wanted to shout, *Mine!*

"My dear, please try to calm yourself. Of course we won't give him the box." Mr. Camel spoke slowly, as if to a wild animal. "But I'm afraid we must leave it here, one last time."

"Leave it?

"We need to get our passports, remember?"

Passports? They were planning on leaving the country. With *my* box.

"But it wants me to protect it," Mrs. Camel said. "I will bring it with us."

"No. Leave it here. The individual forging our documents is a criminal of the lowly variety. Let us not tempt her. The box's powers are strong, as you know, my dear."

Ethan and I stared at each other, equally puzzled. Box's powers?

"But . . ." Mrs. Camel's voice sounded tearful. "How can I leave it again?"

"I will change the combination to ease your concerns," Mr. Camel said. Something clicked. "All is well. The box is safe and sound. And Juniper is tied up tight. After we get our passports, we'll come straight back here, collect the box, and then go force Juniper to tell us how to open it. Let's see how she reacts when we tell her that we are willing to go after her sweet little niece." There was a kissing sound. "Now, why don't you freshen up for the photo."

Oh crud! Ethan and I ducked as low as we could below the tub's rim as Mrs. Camel entered the bathroom. There was only a thin sheet of plastic between me and the woman who'd come up with the evil plan of threatening to hurt me in order to scare my great-aunt. If she decided to take a shower, what would we do? The Swiss army knife was nestled in my pocket but seriously, how would it help? I could con Tyler into taking me to WA DC and I could sneak into a motel room, but no way was I going to stab someone.

Ethan's hand shot to his nose. Hello? This was not the time to get a stress-induced nosebleed.

Water ran in the sink. The towel rod jiggled. A purse unzipped, then zipped again. "You're sure the box is safe?" Mrs. Camel asked as she left the bathroom.

"Only the downtrodden stay in a motel like this. There's nothing here to steal. It is the best kind of hiding place."

A door creaked open. "It had better be the best kind of hiding place," Mrs. Camel said. "There are powers beyond belief in that box."

Another kissing sound followed. "All will be well, my dear. The box will be yours. You will bask in its glory and our reputation will rise from the ashes like a phoenix."

"Yes, like a phoenix."

The door closed and their footsteps faded down the balcony.

"They tied her up," I said. "Did you hear that?" I wanted to scream. Instead, I scrambled out of the tub and ran to the front window. As I peeked out between the curtains, George and Martha Camel walked quickly down the motel staircase, then headed toward the sidewalk. They looked very different without their wigs. Her hair was short and black, while his was a blond buzz cut. Neither seemed old and frail and they were both dressed in jeans and ordinary white shirts. "We have to follow them."

"We don't need to follow them," Ethan said as

he emerged from the bathroom, his head thrown back, a wad of tissue held to his nostrils. "They're going to get passports first, then come back for the box, then go to Juniper." He opened the back window. "Hey, Tyler," he called. "They're gone."

"What did they mean about powers beyond belief?" I asked, trying not to look at the bloodied tissue.

"I don't know. I think they must be crazy." He held the bridge of his nose.

A really bad thought popped into my head. "You don't think it's a weapon, do you?"

"A weapon?" Ethan frowned at me. "Why would Juniper send you a weapon for your birthday?"

"Well, if it holds powers beyond belief, then what else could it be?"

He tossed the tissue into the waste bucket. "If Juniper had a weapon, she'd be a terrorist and we'd need to call Homeland Security, not the police."

"A terrorist?" I might have laughed if the whole thing hadn't been so weird. "Now *we* sound crazy."

Maybe crazy was going around because I couldn't ignore that *feeling*, as if the box was calling to me. I turned on the closet light and knelt next to a small safe. Instructions were posted about how to set the combination, along with a statement saying the motel owner wasn't responsible for stolen items. The tugging feeling grew stronger and stronger. "It's in there," I said, jiggling the handle. I tried to move the safe but it was bolted to the floor. "Do you think we can figure out the combination?"

"I don't know," Ethan said.

The ladder hit the windowsill with a *thunk*. "What is taking so long?" Tyler complained as he climbed. "You expect me to . . . whoa. What's up with the candles and the Greek letters?"

I whipped around. "Greek? You know they're Greek?"

He leaned over the sill. "Yeah. We labeled different sections of Cyclopsville in Greek to make it look authentic. I recognize some of the letters."

"What does it spell?" I asked.

Tyler shrugged. "I don't know. It's Greek to me. Hey, why are you in the closet?"

"Uh . . . Jax wants to break into the safe," Ethan said.

"Break into the safe?" Tyler's face went pale. "Now that's definitely going to look bad on your high-school transcript."

I was ready to plead, beg, throw myself at my cousin's feet if I had to. "Tyler, I need your help. Please. How can I figure out the combination?"

"Math," he said. "Math can solve everything." He climbed into the room, pushed us aside, then lay on his stomach in front of the safe. I almost reminded him that he was now officially breaking and entering, but I didn't. "There are thirty-five input options on the dial, and it's a three-tumbler lock. So that means it's thirty-five to the third, which is forty-two thousand eight hundred seventy-five possible combinations. So, let's assume that I can do roughly seven combinations in a minute. I divide forty-two thousand eight hundred seventy-five by seven and I get six thousand one hundred twenty-five, which is the number of minutes it would take. Then I divide that by sixty to get the number of hours, which is . . . one hundred two." He smiled proudly. "Basic stuff."

"One hundred and two hours?" I asked. "Are you kidding me? You said math can solve everything."

"It can, but I didn't say how long it would take."

Tyler spun the dial.

"Forget math," Ethan said. "Give me my knife." I did. "This is a cheap safe. It's got hinges on the side." With one of the knife's tools, he pushed out the hinge pins and—*voila*—the door fell open. Ethan to the rescue! Relief, cool and crisp, flooded my body. Is this what it felt like to have Gatorade poured over your head after the Super Bowl? Victory was mine!

"You're brilliant," I told him. I squeezed between my cousins, reached in and grabbed the box. It wasn't as shiny as before. The Camels had smudged it with their evil fingerprints. But the surface was still warm.

"I was going to suggest the hinges," Tyler said sheepishly.

While I hugged the box to my chest, a satisfied feeling filled me from the tips of my feet to the top of my head. It was safe. It was back in my arms. Then I looked worriedly at Ethan. "Now how do we save Juniper?"

"Save?" Tyler asked.

I explained. "The Camels are holding her hostage. They have her tied up somewhere. They can't figure out how to open the box so they're going to force her to tell them. They've even threatened to hurt me, if she won't tell them. They said the box contains powers beyond belief. Once they've gotten whatever's inside, they're going to leave the country with fake passports."

"Jeez," Tyler said. "I hate to admit it but maybe my little brother is right. Maybe we should—"

"No," Ethan interrupted. "Don't call the police."

"Huh?" both Tyler and I said.

Ethan began to pace. "Look, we need to help Juniper, right? And we need to keep Jax safe." A plan was spinning in his head. We'd suddenly reversed roles. He was scheming, I was waiting to be told what to do. "If those Camels come back and see a police car sitting outside, they could panic and take off. We might never see Juniper again, and Jax will still have to worry about the Camels coming after her."

I didn't like the sound of that. I had enough trouble shutting off my thoughts at night without adding in the fear of George and Martha Camel kidnapping me. "What do you think we should do?" I asked Ethan.

"Here's what I think," he said, sounding uncharacteristically brave. "You're not going to like this, Jax, but we can trade the box for Juniper. We have it. They want it. And we can tell them how to take the readings and make the circles. Then they can leave the country and we can go home and never see them again."

"Are you serious?" Tyler asked. "After all this, you want to give up the box?"

I ran my hand over the LCD screen. Of course that's what we'd do. We'd trade the box for Juniper. She was our great-aunt and her life was more important than a puzzle box, no matter what was inside. That was the right thing, the only thing to do. But my head felt thick all of sudden, and that tugging feeling was back. I really wanted to keep the box, and the idea of letting it go made my stomach clench. "But what if . . ." I hesitated. Ethan would think that what I was about to say was ridiculous. "What if it does have powers? Powers beyond belief?"

"Uh . . ." Ethan cringed. "You're kidding, right?"

"No, just listen to me." I sat on the edge of the bed and set the box on my lap. My face was reflected back up at me. "I have this weird feeling, and I don't know how to explain it. It's like the box and I belong together. Like I'm supposed to hold on to it. I need to see what's inside."

Ethan let out a long sigh. "Jax, it doesn't matter what's inside. What matters is Juniper's safety and your safety."

"It *does* matter what's inside," I insisted. "That's the whole reason for this trip. The whole reason why Juniper was kidnapped. The whole reason why the Camels are willing to come after me. What if it's something dangerous? Something with power? Some kind of weapon? We can't give it to them. They're horrible people."

"I'm with Jax," Tyler said. "We can't give the box to the Camels." He was standing in front of the strange symbols, staring at his phone. "I just looked these symbols up in the Greek online dictionary." He held out the phone. One word was on the screen.

Pandora.

Sunny Days Motel

To George and Martha Camel,

  We have the box. You have our great-aunt.
  We will meet you in Washington, DC, tomorrow at noon, in front of the White House. There will be lots of people around so don't try anything. We will give you the box in exchange for Juniper. Do not hurt her or you will never see the box again.

  Signed,
  Your worst nightmare

PS: Bring cash to pay for my car window!!!

19
ETHAN

FACT: *The* D *in Washington, DC, stands for* District. *It's called that because it's not a state, but it's still part of this country so it needed to be called something. The* C *stands for* Columbia, *named after Christopher Columbus. People used to be taught that Columbus discovered America and so Columbia was a name used for our country in songs and in poems. Funny how you're taught one thing and it turns out to be a lie. Like a certain man discovering America, or a certain great-aunt not existing.*

We were on our way to the Madison Hotel in DC. Jax's mom called during the drive. Then my mom called. We didn't have to lie too much. We said we'd made a lot of stops along the way and that we were almost there. My nose tingled after each conversation, but I made it through. Good thing I wasn't Pinocchio.

During the ride from the Sunny Days Motel, I sat in the front seat so I could help with directions. Even with Tyler's weird music, which now sounded like monks chanting, Jax managed to fall into a deep sleep in the backseat. She kept a tight grip on the box the whole time. This had been the craziest day ever.

What we'd decided was this—we'd trade the box for Juniper, the *empty* box. Jax and Tyler were determined to keep whatever was inside. So we just had to be a bit sneaky, and not let them know the box had been opened until Juniper was safe.

"It doesn't exist," I said.

Tyler chewed on an apple core. "What are you talking about?"

"I know what you're thinking. You're thinking about the word on the wall. You're thinking about Pandora's box. But it's not real."

The monks stopped chanting. I knew the song had ended but it seemed like they'd paused the music so they could listen to our conversation.

"Of course it's just a story." Tyler glanced warily at me, then we both looked quickly over our shoulders at the metal box on Jax's lap. A whining sound arose as Tyler's car veered over the yellow line. He cursed and quickly turned his attention back to the road. "But haven't you heard that fact is often stranger than fiction?"

I know about facts. They clog my brain. They are real. Pandora wasn't any more real than Santa Claus.

As twilight fell over the city, we finally reached the Madison Hotel, which was four blocks from the White House. I'd chosen the White House as the location for our "exchange" because I figured there would be lots of security guards around and we'd be safe. I nudged Jax until she woke up. Tyler pulled up to the entrance and a valet took the car keys. This had been one of the instructions during Mom's lecture that morning. "Have the valet park the car. There's a lot of crime in our nation's capital and the valet will put the car in a secure garage." And, as Mom knew, with the valet helping, Tyler wouldn't have to parallel park.

We checked in at the front desk, then carried our backpacks so we wouldn't have to pay a bellhop. Jax was still groggy as we rode up in the elevator, but the moment we stepped into the room, her eyes widened. "Wow," she said. "This is amazing."

Tyler and I had done a lot of traveling with our parents, so we'd seen our fair share of hotel rooms, but this was super nice, not because the two queen beds had satin covers or because there was a vase of fresh flowers and bottles of chilled water, but because the flat-screen TV was double the size of our TV at home.

Tyler immediately claimed the desk, set up his laptop and gaming mouse, and logged into the hotel's wireless.

"Look at the bathroom," Jax said.

One bathroom wall was totally covered in mirrors. A basket stuffed with mini shampoo bottles, lotion, soap, and shower caps sat on the marble counter. And the toilet was one of those Japanese toilets I'd read about in *Wired* magazine, that squirts water and then blows hot air to dry your butt. "Cool," I said.

"I love these towels," Jax said, running her hands over one. "They're so fluffy."

The bathtub was big enough for two people. Not

that we were going to take a bath together. We hadn't done that since we were babies. How many times had Mom embarrassed me with those photos?

Tyler opened the mini fridge. "Look at all this stuff. Cheese, pâté, candy—there's even wine and beer in here." He grabbed a package of crackers. My stomach growled but I first had to call Mom. "We're here," I told her. I assured her that Tyler had driven safely, no speeding, and that the hotel was nice. Then came the part I hated—the lying. "We'll check into the geocaching event tomorrow." Jax was resting on the bed, her eyes closed, the box nestled on her lap. I turned my back to her and whispered into the phone. "Mom, do you know if we have any . . . terrorists in the family?"

"What?" Mom asked.

"Uh . . . anyone who builds or trades weapons?"

"Those are very strange questions, Ethan. And why are you whispering? I can barely hear you."

"I'm just wondering if . . . well, if we have anyone in the family who might be . . ."

"Are you asking about Juniper again?"

"No." The lie felt heavy on my tongue, and when I swallowed, it felt like I'd swallowed a boulder.

Mom's voice tightened. "Your Aunt Lindsay told

me that Jax got a birthday present from Juniper. The present was taken away for good reason. I don't want you to ask any more questions about her. It would make your Aunt Lindsay very upset."

"Okay."

What had begun as a simple plan to open a birthday box had turned into something dangerous, with sinister overtones. It felt more like a movie than real life. Mom, Dad, and Aunt Lindsay knew things about Juniper, things that might help us deal with the Camels. Things that might help us figure out what was inside the box. I glanced over at Jax. Her chest rose and fell with deep breaths. "Mom," I said. "Can you call Aunt Lindsay? Jax is real sleepy from the drive. Can you tell her we've checked in and we're okay?"

"Sure. Give your brother a kiss for me." Tyler was online, his butt firmly glued to the hotel chair, his headphones in place. He'd kicked off his shoes and socks and a sour odor had already begun to fill the room.

"I'm not giving Tyler a kiss."

"I don't know why you two can't be nice to each other. One day, when your father and I are long gone, you'll appreciate having a brother."

"I'm still not giving him a kiss."

"Fine. Call me in the morning. Bye."

I kicked Tyler's disgusting shoes and socks into the closet, then I ordered room service—cheeseburgers, fries, and lemonades. They arrived on big trays with miniature ketchup bottles and tiny salt and pepper shakers. The smell of toasted bun and melted cheese woke up Jax. Tyler grabbed his plate and set it next to the computer. I took all the green stuff off of Jax's plate before handing it to her.

"They've probably found the note by now," I said as I sprinkled salt on my fries. "Do you think we did the right thing?"

"Yes," Jax said. Her eyes were puffy. She looked like she hadn't slept in ages. "We have the box. It's going to be okay."

I nodded. Of course, I wasn't so sure. I'd never done anything like this before. And a big question was nagging at me—what would happen if we opened the box and discovered something dangerous?

After tossing my baseball cap aside and slipping off my Converse shoes, I sat cross-legged on the bed. Jax sat cross-legged too, the plates between us. That's the cool thing about staying in a hotel room without your parents—if you get ketchup on the bedspread, they can't yell at you about it.

"Juniper was smiling at me in that photo, the one where she was holding me when I was a baby." Jax thumped the ketchup bottle. The puzzle box was wedged between her and a pillow. "She looks like a nice person."

I hoped she was a nice person, because a nice person wouldn't put something dangerous into a box and mail it to her niece. Tyler jammed fries into his mouth and mumbled something at the screen. My eyelids had begun to feel heavy but the food reenergized me. It had the same effect on Jax. She crammed her cheeks like a chipmunk and her eyes brightened.

"I say we press the button," she said after gulping the last of her lemonade.

"Here? Are you sure? We can only push the button two more times."

"We're in the center of DC. This is as good a place as any. Besides, we're kind of running on luck now."

Tyler was wearing his headphones, so he had no idea what we were talking about. "Ambush!" he cried as the screen lit up with bursts of weapon fire. His fingers danced across the gaming mouse as he perched at the edge of his chair.

I expected Jax to tell Tyler what we were about to do. But she didn't. "Just you and me," she said.

Nice to know I was still her partner.

After getting the map, ruler, and protractor from my backpack, I followed Jax out onto the balcony. Evening had bled into night. The city was all lit up. A bar was playing loud music. We could see into the windows where people were laughing and dancing. The day's heat had faded but it was still warm enough for shorts. Below the balcony, headlights glided like lanterns on a river. Jax held the box up to the sky. "I want to make sure I get a good signal."

"Uh . . . what if we're wrong?" I asked. "What if the right spot isn't in DC but it's in the middle of Lake Oneida? What if we came all this way and—"

"We're not wrong," Jax said. Then, with a smile, she pushed the button. Light arose from the screen. She lowered the box so we could read.

Attempt 9 of 10.
1.8 miles from the right spot.
Good-bye.

"We're soooo close," she whispered. "So, so, so close."

"Great," I said, only somewhat happy. Part of me had wanted to fail, so we could go home and be done with this.

The map I'd brought wouldn't help us because it didn't show enough detail. So I found a DC city map in a stack of tourist information in the room. We sat side by side on the balcony, the map spread out. After marking our location at the Madison Hotel, I measured the radius of 1.8 miles, then drew the circle. The circle ran through streets, parks and buildings. "It could be any of these locations," I said.

"I don't think Juniper would choose just any old place. Think about it. She's an archaeologist so she's all about relics and treasures." Jax's finger traced the circle. It clipped the edge of the Museum of Natural History. "That's a possibility," she said. The circle crossed roads and parks, then went straight through the center of a building.

"The Lincoln Memorial," I said.

Jax's eyes widened. "Hello? That has to be the right spot. That photo showed Juniper and me at the Lincoln Memorial."

I nodded. It made sense.

"I have a good feeling about this," Jax said. "And it's important to listen to your feelings."

"Uh . . . you mean like when I had those feelings that we should call the police? You didn't listen to those."

"That's because they weren't *my* feelings." She gave me a teasing smile. Then she looked up at the night sky. "We can't go now, it's too late." I sighed with relief, because I'd thought for sure she'd make us go out in the dark and trek through a city known for its monuments *and* its crime. "We'll go first thing in the morning."

Using her sleeve, she began to polish the box. I could understand why she wanted to keep it. The design was amazing. The seams weren't visible, and the LCD screen was so perfectly placed, it looked like it melted into the shiny metal. "Do you remember the Camels saying that someone named the Locksmith built the box?"

"Yeah, I remember. They also said that no one knows where he is." Jax's face suddenly went dark and she stopped polishing. "Do you think she's afraid?"

"Who?"

"Great-Aunt Juniper. Do you think she's still tied up? Do you think she's scared?"

"I'd be scared," I said. "But they won't hurt her. They want the box. It'll be okay." Strange, but Jax was the one who was worried and I was the one doing the comforting. What I didn't say was this—remember that evil voice on the phone? He wants the box, too. "Let's get some sleep."

While Tyler's alter ego wandered through the bowels of a virtual labyrinth, fighting with a half-man, half-bull creature, Jax and I climbed into opposite beds. I won't go into detail but that Japanese toilet was weird. I grabbed the tourist guidebook and read about the Lincoln Memorial. Reading helps quiet my mind when it's spinning. My parents would kill me if they knew that tomorrow I was going to make a hostage exchange.

Jax started to snore and my eyelids grew heavy again. I turned off all the lights until the only glow came from Tyler's computer. As I pulled back the sheets, Tyler whipped around. "That's my bed. I claim it."

"But I got it first."

"Oh yeah?" He pulled off his headphones, scrambled out of the chair and grabbed one of his dirty socks from the closet. Then he rubbed the sock all over the sheets and pillow. "Do you still want this bed?" he asked with a smirk.

We were kids again, fighting over the best sleeping

bag, or the best place on the couch. He'd always be older and bigger so he'd always get the good stuff. "Fine!" What a jerk.

I climbed into bed next to Jax, careful not to wake her. The box was tucked under the covers, taking up a lot of room. It jabbed my arm with its sharp corner. I tried to move it, gently tugging it free of her grip, but she opened one eye and stared at me. "What are you doing?"

"The box is in the way."

She sat up, suddenly wide awake, her hair matted to one side of her face. "Then go sleep in the other bed."

"I'm not going to sleep with Tyler. He rubbed his disgusting sock all over the sheets. Can't you just move the box?"

She clutched it to her chest. "Don't try to take it," she said, "or you'll be sorry."

"I'll be sorry? What's that supposed to mean?"

She looked at me, her eyes flashing like a warning sign. "Those who cross the protector will suffer." She turned her back to me, the box tucked beneath the covers. Then she started snoring again.

"Whatever," I mumbled. What a grouch! Maybe she just needed sleep. I grabbed a pillow and blanket and found a spot on the carpet.

But something didn't feel right, and Jax was always saying that you shouldn't ignore a feeling. Was it that look in her eyes when she'd said she was the protector of the box? Or the way she'd spoken in a monotone, like a robot?

Those who cross the protector will suffer.

20
JAX

Tuesday

I was stuck in one of Tyler's games.

They came at me from all sides. Clutching my box, I ran up and down staircases, through dark passages, between ancient ruins. Everywhere I went, people reached out their hands, trying to grab my treasure. Mr. Camel darted around a pillar, his eyes blazing like campfires. Mrs. Camel jumped out of a crypt like a jack-in-the-box, her twitchy fingers as long as rulers. Tyler blasted his way toward me with a ray gun. I threw myself behind a stone wall. Ethan stood in a doorway, waving at me, smiling. "Come on in, Jax. Don't worry. You'll be safe with me." I staggered toward him, knowing he'd protect me. I could trust Ethan. He'd never deceive me.

But when I got close to the door, he stepped aside and the Camels were right behind him.

"Give us the box!"

I woke up coated with sweat, my heart racing. The bed wasn't mine. The comforter wasn't mine. Where was I?

It took a moment for my eyes to adjust. Our room at the Madison Hotel was faintly lit by the glow of Tyler's computer. He'd fallen asleep at the desk. Ethan lay asleep on the carpet, burrowed beneath a blanket, a mop of brown hair sticking out. I felt around the bed. Where was it? My heart skipped a beat. Where . . . ? As soon as my fingers found the smooth surface, I exhaled.

The only other time I'd felt this way about an object was when I was really little. Spot, my stuffed orca whale, had gone everywhere with me. He came from the zoo's gift shop and I'm not sure why I'd latched on to him. Why does one kid carry a blanket around and another kid carry an orca whale? Spot went to restaurants, movie theaters—he even took baths with me. When I couldn't find him because Mom had put him in the dryer, or because I'd dropped him in the driveway, I'd get an achy feeling and it wouldn't go away until he was in my arms. Eventually Spot lost all his stuffing and turned into a tattered piece of fabric, but by that time I'd grown up and didn't need him anymore.

Now I needed something else.

The box lay safely beside me, under the covers. The Camels had tried to steal it. Tyler and Ethan each wanted a third. Everyone was trying to cheat me out of my rightful birthday present—conspiring, ganging up on me. Why should I share?

With the sheet's edge, I wiped sweat from my face. What was wrong with me? Why was I having all these dark thoughts? *Get a grip*, I told myself. *You're losing it!*

After quietly sliding out of bed and stepping around Ethan, I carried the box into the bathroom and got a glass of water. My reflection stared back at me, dark circles under my eyes, hair frizzed out like a Brillo pad. Using the little bar of soap from the basket, I washed my face. The warm water didn't calm my thoughts. I tried cold water but I still felt weird.

I pulled my hair into a ponytail and looked into the mirror again. My thoughts felt thick, like they were floating in pudding. Weren't we supposed to do something today? Oh right. Juniper. We were supposed to rescue our great-aunt.

I am the protector of the box.

Yes, the protector. Juniper's name faded away and all I could sense was the box. It had been given to me and it was my duty to keep it safe. The contents were for my eyes only. Ethan and Tyler had no right to claim a third. I'd sneak out and open it on my own.

I put on my purple jacket, then carefully set the precious box into my backpack, wedged safely between a shirt and an extra pair of jeans. Keep it hidden. Keep it safe.

Tyler was still slumped over the desk, wrappers from the minibar scattered around him. His shirt expanded with his steady breaths. Ethan was still curled under the blanket. Was I doing the right thing? Tyler would be pissed when he found out I'd tried to open the box without him. Ethan might not care about what was inside, but he'd feel left out, that's for sure. I didn't want to hurt his feelings. He'd been my partner in most everything. I'd convinced him to go on this trip and yet, there I stood, ready to sneak out without him.

I reached out to wake him but hesitated. Dream images flashed through my mind—the Camels with their greedy hands, Tyler and his ray gun, Ethan trying to lure me into a trap. His Swiss army knife lay on the floor next to his wallet. I grabbed the knife and stuck it into my pocket.

Those who cross the protector will suffer.

No one could be trusted. I had to do this alone. Creeping like a cat burglar, I silently opened the door and stepped into the hall. With a gentle *click* the door closed. Morning newspapers lay along the hallway. Room-service trays from last night were piled on a housekeeping cart. The stairs would be faster than waiting for the elevator. I dashed down, stopping a few times, listening to make sure no one was following.

People with suitcases sat in the hotel lobby, waiting near a sign that read, *Airport Van Pickup*. Nine A.M., according to the lobby clock. I must have been really tired to have slept so long. "What's the best way to get to the Lincoln Memorial?" I asked a guy who was working the reception desk. He told me what to do, then drew the directions on a walking map. After I thanked him, he looked at me funny. Then he stared at my backpack. My stomach clenched. Did he know about the box? How was that possible? I grabbed the map and hurried out of the hotel.

The morning sun was so bright it made me wince. The street buzzed with traffic. After taking a right, I stood on the corner of Fifteenth and M Streets NW. The directions had me heading south down Fifteenth, crossing L Street, K Street, and I Street. Who'd come up with such boring street names? I pressed the crosswalk button and waited. Bouncing on my toes, come on, come on. Change the light. There was too much traffic to dart across. If I had my bike I could be so much faster. As soon as I reached the memorial, I'd open the box and claim the prize for myself. Keeping it safe from everyone else.

Protect. The. Box.

"Jax, where are you going?"

It was Ethan's voice. I turned on my heels. He and Tyler stood behind me on the sidewalk, in the same clothes they'd worn all day yesterday and had slept in. Tyler's stubble was turning to beard.

"She's sneaking off," Tyler said, crossing his arms. "She's going to open it without us."

I clamped my fingers around the backpack straps. "It's *my* birthday present. I can do whatever I want with it."

"We all know it's *your* birthday present," Tyler said. "That's not in contention. But must I remind you, little cousin, that if we end up selling whatever's in that box, you agreed to give me one third."

"No," I said. "I don't want to."

"Uh . . . Jax?" Ethan stepped closer and as he did, I stepped away. "You look different. Are you sick? Your face is red."

"Stay away from me." I took another step, my heel balancing on the sidewalk's edge. "I know you want to take it from me and keep it for yourself."

"Huh?" Ethan pushed hair from his eyes. "Why would I do that?"

I couldn't answer his question. Part of me knew I wasn't making sense. Ethan had never stolen a single thing, not even a candy bar. The only times he'd gotten into trouble were because of me. So why would he, all of a sudden, do something to hurt me? He wouldn't. But as soon as I convinced myself that Ethan was no threat, my gut tightened and my head filled with dark thoughts. He can't be trusted. Protect the box.

"Just leave me alone." I turned and darted into the road. A taxi honked and swerved. A car slammed its brakes.

"Jax!" Ethan yelled, but I was already across the intersection.

Down Fifteenth I ran, making the walk lights with perfect timing, which could have been pure luck but I knew it was fate. I was meant to open the box. The contents were mine.

A block over, I stopped for a moment to check the map. I'd reached Lafayette Park, a big green area, and I was supposed to cross it and make my way around the White House. I ran past a giant statue of a man riding a horse. Tourists were everywhere, holding up their cell phones and clicking photos. I didn't stop to gawk at the White House. This wasn't a sightseeing trip.

I came to a big slab. The sign read, *Zero Milestone*.

"Wait!" Ethan caught up and grabbed my arm. He could barely talk, he was breathing so hard. "Why are you running so fast?"

I yanked my arm away. Tyler was in the distance, his pace slowing. "Don't worry," Ethan said.

"He'll take forever to get here. This is the most exercise he's gotten in years. Now tell me what's wrong. Jax?" He looked into my eyes.

"I need to do this alone." I started running again. Ethan followed.

"I won't let you face the Camels on your own. They're too dangerous."

Camels?

"Go away," I told him, trying to race ahead. But he stubbornly kept up with me.

"Why are you acting like this?" he asked. "I know Tyler's a pain in the butt, but you made a deal with him. He drove us here, remember? And we need him when the Camels come. He might not be able to run very fast but he's a big guy."

I am the protector of the box.

We crossed Constitution Avenue, just like the man had told me. The right spot wasn't far. "Hey, that's the Washington Monument. Slow down, would you? I'm getting a side ache." Ethan grabbed me around the waist and pulled me to a stop. "Why are you always in a hurry?"

I was about to twist free of Ethan's grip when the world went silent. No hum of traffic. No gasps as Ethan tried to catch his breath. Tourists stood in clumps, talking, but I couldn't hear their voices. Eyes turned toward me, staring at my backpack. I slid out of the straps and hugged it to my chest. A few people slowed down, looking, looking, looking. How could they know about the box? How could I protect it from this many people? It was just me. Me against all of them. How could I . . . ?

Someone ripped the backpack from my hands.

Tyler had swooped in like a vulture. His face was all sweaty but victory shined in his eyes. I took a deep breath, about to scream, about to punch him when . . .

. . . I unfurled my fists. Sound returned. A car honked. A baby cried. A woman in high heels clicked past. The world cleared as if I'd been walking through fog and it had suddenly lifted. Relief washed over me. The backpack had felt like dead weight and my shoulders ached where the straps had rubbed. Tourists no longer stared. They walked past, minding their own business, caught up in their own plans. No one was trying to steal the box. My two cousins gazed at me, bewildered. I rubbed my eyes. "What's going on?"

"What's going on?" Tyler asked sarcastically. "You totally freaked out."

"I . . . I thought you and Ethan wanted to steal the box," I told him.

"How could you think that?" Ethan's voice cracked. "When have I ever stolen anything from you?"

Never. That was the answer. Ethan was the most trustworthy person I knew. What was wrong with me? "I'm sorry. I don't know why I felt that way. It doesn't make any sense. As soon as you took the backpack, I didn't feel like that anymore."

"You called yourself the protector," Ethan said. He shoved his hands into his plaid pockets.

I didn't know how to explain the way I'd acted, so I changed the subject. "Where's your hat?" I asked. It was so weird to see him without it.

"I ran out of the hotel so fast I forgot it," he said. "Jax? You looked right at me and called yourself the protector of the box."

"Yeah, I guess I did." I cringed. "That sounds crazy, doesn't it? But I wanted to protect it, more than anything."

"It's like the ring," Tyler said, his voice mysterious.

"What ring?" I asked.

He motioned us over to a bench, where we sat

very close, me in the middle. Then he lowered his voice, as if about to tell a scary story around a campfire. "The One Ring, Sauron's ring. From J. R. R. Tolkien's epic, *The Lord of the Rings.*" Ignoring Ethan's groan, Tyler launched into an explanation. "The One Ring contained the dark powers of Sauron, an evil being who wanted to dominate Middle Earth. When Frodo Baggins wore the ring, he was consumed by dark thoughts and suspected everyone around him of trying to steal it. So he tried to sneak away without the other members of his fellowship following."

"Give us a break," Ethan said with a huge roll of his eyes. "Are you saying that Jax is like Frodo and that her birthday box is like Sauron's ring?"

"Maybe." Tyler shrugged. "Why not? Jax has been holding the box ever since we got it out of the motel safe. She even slept with it. Then she tried to sneak away. Frodo believed that he was the protector of the ring. Jax believes that she's the protector of the box."

Usually I'd ignore Tyler's fantasies, but something felt true. "I heard Mrs. Camel say the same thing. She said that the box wanted her to protect it. And Mr. Camel said that the powers were strong."

Tyler raised an eyebrow. "And don't forget that the Camels wrote *Pandora* on the motel-room wall. Pandora's box was full of evil, just like Sauron's ring."

These stories were beginning to sound oddly familiar. I lowered my voice. "I had strange dreams that everyone was trying to take the box, including both of you. And even though it didn't make any sense, I knew I needed to sneak away. It was as if the box was telling me to sneak away. I couldn't control my feelings."

We all looked at the backpack.

"Mind control," Tyler whispered.

"Okay, you two are just trying to freak me out," Ethan said, rising from the bench. "This is ridiculous. Pandora is a Greek myth. Sauron is a villain from a book. Whatever's inside the box is worth money and the Camels want it. They are greedy thieves, that's all. Let's just go open the stupid thing, get Juniper back, and go home. I'm sick of this quest." He grabbed the backpack and slung it over a shoulder. "And let's get one thing straight. Next time you want a partner for one of your stupid adventures, ask someone else!"

21
ETHAN

FACT: *Older brothers who spend most of their free time cutting the heads off of Cyclopses are completely out of touch with reality.*

I didn't believe a word. How could a box have powers? Jax got greedy, that was the truth. She didn't want to share. She tried to do this without us but we caught her so she came up with this story about dark feelings. Tyler hadn't surprised me—he was always talking about one of his games or fantasy novels. But Jax had acted like I wasn't trustworthy. I'd never taken anything from her. I'd been her loyal sidekick time and time again. But instead of apologizing, she'd blamed her actions on the box, as if it had power over her. And Tyler had agreed, with his idiotic suggestion about mind control.

Mind control? No one was controlling my mind. Not anymore. Those two could play their games but I was done with this whole thing. As soon as Juniper was safe, I'd go home and find something to do that didn't include great-aunts, kidnappers, or anything Greek.

The Lincoln Memorial stood at the other end of the Reflecting Pool, a rectangular pond that was more than one third of a mile long. The memorial's image floated on the pool's glass-like surface. I didn't share interesting facts with either Tyler or Jax. They wouldn't care that to the right was the Constitution Garden, and that the large black wall was the Vietnam Veterans Memorial. But if I said, *Oh look, there's a hobbit*, they'd be interested.

I stopped walking. The Lincoln Memorial awaited us, gleaming white against the perfectly green lawn that surrounded it. A wide set of stairs led up to the twelve pillars that flanked the memorial's entrance. We stood, Tyler on my right, Jax on my left, gazing upward. "I feel like I'm in ancient Greece," Jax said.

"That's because it was built to look like a Greek

Doric temple," I told her, my frustration fading. This place was amazing. I felt like I'd gone back in time. "It was a controversial building. Many people thought it was too fancy and didn't represent President Lincoln's humble character. They wanted a log cabin instead." I'd read about it in the tourist brochure.

We walked up the steps, between a pair of pillars, and entered the monument. It was quiet inside, as if we'd stepped onto sacred ground. I'd seen photos of the Lincoln statue, but none of them compared to the real thing. It was like coming face-to-face with a giant. He towered over us from his throne, his features rugged, his eyes gentle. Above him the following words were inscribed:

IN THIS TEMPLE
AS IN THE HEARTS OF THE PEOPLE
FOR WHOM HE SAVED THE UNION
THE MEMORY OF ABRAHAM
LINCOLN IS ENSHRINED FOREVER.

"Saved the union," Jax whispered.

"Some experts believe that as many as seven hundred thousand Americans were killed in the Civil War," I whispered back. "Imagine if that happened today. What if the East Coast decided to go to war against the West Coast?"

"Hey, that's a great idea for a game," Tyler said, nudging my arm. "I'm going to call Walker." He whipped out his phone but a security guard shook his head. This was not the place to make calls. Tyler sheepishly slid his phone back into his pocket.

Though the box waited, we were caught up in the moment. A tour guide walked past, giving a presentation to a group wearing matching T-shirts. The tour guide was delivering a long list of facts about the height and width of the statue, the type of marble, and a bunch of dates.

My brain was overloaded with all the stuff I'd read last night. "You see the way his hands are posed," I said to Jax and Tyler. "No one knows for sure if the sculptor meant to do this, but the fingers of his left hand form the letter *A* in sign language, and the fingers of his right hand form the letter *L*, his initials."

A person from the tour group stopped. "Is that true?" he asked me.

I felt my face go red. I reached for my baseball cap, so I could hide beneath the brim, but it wasn't there. I looked at my feet. "Uh . . . well, yes, it is true. The fingers form those letters."

Another person stopped. She had a foreign accent. "Vhy is zee statue so big?"

I wanted to turn away, but she was waiting for my answer. The tour guide had also stopped and all the people in the matching T-shirts were watching me. "Uh . . ." I swallowed. "Well, the statue was only supposed to be ten feet tall but that would have made Lincoln look small, compared to such a large room. So they changed it to nineteen feet. Lincoln's only surviving son, Robert, got to see the statue when the memorial opened in 1922. He liked it."

The tour guide smiled curtly at me, then clapped his hands. "This way folks. Follow me."

Tyler patted my shoulder. "You know, little brother, I think we may have just found a career for you." There wasn't a hint of sarcasm in his voice. It was the nicest thing he'd ever said to me.

"I can't believe you talked in front of all those people." Jax put her arm around me. "That was amazing. I'm so sorry I acted like an idiot. I know you'd never take the box. You're my best friend."

It might have been one of those awkward moments, but Tyler in his usual annoyed tone said, "Are we just going to stand here and talk about how much we *love* each other, or are we going to open the box?"

We didn't dare open a backpack inside the monument, not with all the security guards standing watch. So we walked back outside and around the building until we found a spot of shade next to one of the pillars. Tyler sat against the stone; Jax and I sat crisscross facing him. I opened the backpack and took out the box. The metal was slightly warm, as if a freshly baked cookie lay inside. I set it on the ground between us and then looked at Jax. "You should be the one to press it," I told her.

She moved her finger toward the button, then pulled away, her expression uncertain. "What if I touch it and get those weird thoughts again?"

"Jax," I said calmly. "It's a box. It's made of metal. It can't give you bad thoughts."

"What if it can?" Tyler asked.

I groaned. He was absolutely no help. I could tell by her clenched lips that Tyler's story about Sauron and the ring had freaked her out.

"I'll do it," I said.

And I pushed the button.

22
JAX

When I first pushed the button back home in Chatham, New Jersey, I wasn't biting my lip with fear. My heart wasn't pounding in my ears. I'd expected the lid to pop open and inside there'd be a Starbucks gift card or something else that was totally normal. But nothing about this birthday present was normal. The box had changed my dreams, had changed my feelings. Ethan could deny it but he hadn't been inside my head. He hadn't felt the darkness roll through my thoughts.

No one was watching us. People strolled around the memorial. Sunlight fell upon the stone, brightening it like a new coat of white paint. If all the tourists suddenly disappeared it would be easy to pretend that we were back in ancient Greece, temple pillars towering above our heads. The only things missing were our togas and sandals.

This was it. The moment when we'd discover whether we'd succeeded or failed. The box would open and reveal its secret. Or not. As Ethan pushed the button, I held my breath.

The screen lit up.

Final Attempt.

Then it went dark. And stayed dark. No more words appeared.

Hello? Why didn't it open? We'd failed. My shoulders sank as if weighed down by boulders. I wanted to lie on the stone floor and cry. *I'm sorry*, I thought. *I'm sorry, Juniper.* Tears stung my eyes. "You said geometry would solve it," I snapped at Tyler. "We did what you said. We made the circles."

"What? You're blaming this on me?"

I needed to blame it on someone, because if I didn't, the disappointment would well up and I'd explode. And besides, Tyler just happened to be sitting next to me. "I'm totally blaming it on you," I said, folding my arms. "You said math solves everything."

"That's just great." Tyler got to his feet. "I take time out of my precious schedule to drive you all over the planet and you blame this on me. I'm not the one who did the readings."

"Open," I ordered the box. "Open, open, open!" I wanted to shake it, but if I touched it those dark feelings would come again. "Open!"

"Uh . . . Jax?" Ethan looked around. "People can hear you."

So what if I was acting like a baby? The stupid box wasn't cooperating. I leaned against the pillar, folded my arms, and squeezed my eyes shut. "This isn't fair."

"Jax?" Ethan scooted closer. "Please don't start sulking. I hate it when you do that. We still have to save Juniper."

"Leave me alone," I grumbled.

"Whatever," Tyler said. "Once again, this quest totally sucks. I'm going to go find a Starbucks. My life points are low. I need some major caffeine." He started to walk away.

"Look," Ethan said with a gasp. "There's a new message."

"What?" My eyes flew open. The screen had lit up again. Tyler sat back down and we all drew quick, excited breaths.

Congratulations, Jax. You have found the right spot.

A shiver darted across my shoulder blades. The box knew my name. This was the proof that it wasn't supposed to be opened by Mr. or Mrs. Camel, or by the owner of the evil voice. It was meant for me.

Click. A red light appeared, like a pinprick in the box's corner. Then the light began to move along the edge like a flame and as it did so, it left a thin crack. It ran around three sides, then stopped. The light extinguished.

Before anyone said a word, Tyler's hand darted out and he opened the lid. We leaned forward so quickly that Ethan and I knocked heads. "Ouch," he said, rubbing beneath his bangs.

The pain was sharp but I didn't care. "What is

it?" I asked, still afraid to touch the box.

"There's a note," Tyler said.

We leaned close. I recognized the same handwriting that I'd seen on Juniper's photos.

Dear Jax,

DO NOT open this jar under any circumstances. It is extremely dangerous. DO NOT sell this jar, no matter how much money is offered to you. Protect it. Keep it safe until I arrive. If you do not hear from me within a year's time, drop the jar to the bottom of the ocean and forget it ever existed.

With sincerely kind thoughts,

Your Great-Aunt Juniper Vandegrift

"Protect it," I read. "I was right. I am the protector of the box."

"A jar that's extremely dangerous?" Ethan reread the letter. "This sounds bad. Really bad."

Tyler pulled out something that was covered in bubble wrap. It was small enough to hold in one hand. Carefully, he peeled back the wrap. And there, in his palm, lay the little black clay jar, decorated with white swirls. The top was sealed with a plug that was also made from clay. Tyler moved it to his other hand.

"Careful, don't break it," I said.

"I'm not going to break it," Tyler said. "But it's making my hand sweaty."

"What do you mean?" I asked.

"It's hot," he said. "Real hot."

Both Ethan and I touched the pot. My fingers sizzled with heat, as if a fire burned inside the clay. "So that's why the metal box was always warm," I realized. "But why?"

"Uh . . ." Ethan quickly withdrew his hand. "Remember how back in the motel room you wondered if it might be a weapon of some kind?" I nodded. "Only three elements produce heat— potassium, thorium, and uranium. All three are radioactive."

"Radioactive?" I gasped.

Tyler quickly set the jar on the ground, then we all scooted away.

"Why would Juniper send me a radioactive pot? She can't send radioactive stuff through the mail, can she? Don't they check for that sort of thing at the post office?" Ethan and Tyler both shrugged.

There had to be another explanation. "Maybe the jar is hot because it was trapped inside the box. It's a hot day." What else could it be? If Juniper had sent me a radioactive pot, then that would make her a terrible evil person and that would make us culprits in some kind of weapons deal.

Ethan took out his phone and began to type. "I remember reading about an app . . ." He typed some more. "Here it is. I'm downloading it now."

"Ethan? This is important. Stop playing with your phone." I couldn't believe it.

"Wait, this might work." He typed some more, then held his phone over the jar. "The app uses the camera feature to detect radioactivity. Radioactivity creates current that disrupts the camera feature, and will show up as bright spots." Ethan moved the phone around the pot. "Nothing," he reported. "No radioactivity."

"Phew," I said. "That's a relief."

Ethan slid the phone into the pocket of his plaid shorts. "I was just thinking how bad it would be if we'd been carrying around a radioactive box for the past two days. Radiation poisoning is serious. We read about it in history class. You get vomiting, fever, bloody diarrhea, and then you die."

"So now that we know it's not going to liquefy our bowels, how about we open it," Tyler said. He reached for the clay plug but I grabbed his hand.

"Wait." I said. "The note says don't open it."

"What?" Spit sprayed from Tyler's mouth. "Don't open it? We came all this way and now you don't want to open it?"

"We can't ignore the note. And besides, I have a feeling."

"Another feeling?" Tyler scowled. "Why don't you just admit it, Jax? You want to open it without us. You tried to sneak away and keep it for yourself because you don't want to share."

"Uh . . . you'd better stop arguing," Ethan said. "Look."

I spun around. Mr. and Mrs. Camel were walking along the edge of the sprawling lawn. Mr. Camel held onto another woman's arm. She was too far away to make out her features but her hair hung in two long white braids, and a red bandana was wound around her neck.

"Great-Aunt Juniper," I whispered.

23

JAX

The Camels hadn't noticed us. We scooted behind the pillar, then watched from the shadows as they walked around to the front of the memorial.

"What are they doing here? We told them to meet us at the White House." Ethan checked his phone. "It's nowhere near noon."

"Juniper must have told them where to open the box," I realized. "They came early to try to catch us off guard. But they're too late. Juniper's note said to protect the jar and that's what I'm going to do."

Though I was scared to touch it, I picked up the jar. The heat sizzled my fingertips and I felt a surge of darkness. Everything around me changed as suspicion filled my mind. It was like putting a special-effects lens on a camera. No longer had the tourists come to see the Lincoln Memorial—they'd come to get my prize. They stared at me. They whispered to each other about how they'd steal it. Tyler and Ethan were sitting close enough to grab it. I wanted to run from everyone, get far away and protect it—

"Jax?" Ethan said. "Your face is turning red."

I set the jar onto the sheet of bubble wrap. The minute I let it go, the lens was lifted and the dark thoughts disappeared. "Could you do it?" I told Ethan. "Could you rewrap it and set it into my backpack?" Ethan did. "Could you carry it?" I asked Tyler. Because for some reason, the jar didn't give him or Ethan the same dark feelings.

"Sure." Tyler slid his arms through the straps.

I picked up the box. There was no way we could pretend that it hadn't been opened. The seam was visible, even with the lid closed. And the metal was cold, lifeless. This was going to be tricky.

I redid my ponytail, then took a deep breath. "Okay, here we go. Remember, don't act suspicious. Tell yourself that there's nothing inside the backpack. If you act like you're carrying something special, the Camels will notice." Tyler nodded.

"Uh-oh." Ethan's hand flew to his nose.

"Don't stress out," I told him. "We can do this." Ethan's hand trembled slightly. I was trembling, too, but doing a better job at hiding it. All those times I'd taken risks, all those times I'd broken rules—where was my confidence now? "We'll make the exchange on the steps, right in front of the security guards. The Camels wouldn't dare hurt any of us." It sounded like a solid plan. What could go wrong?

How about *everything*?

We walked around to the front of the memorial and took our places on the wide steps. I stood in the middle, holding the box. Tyler stood on my left, gripping the backpack straps. Ethan stood on my right, pinching the bridge of his nose. The tourist crowd had doubled in size. Across the street, the Reflecting Pool sparkled as sunshine danced on its surface. A trio of street musicians played steel drums in the distance.

As visitors walked past, tugging on the arms of tired, hungry children, I felt like I was in some kind of movie. A few days ago I'd been celebrating my twelfth birthday, wondering what I was going to do all summer, and there I was, trying to protect a sizzling-hot jar that contained something dangerous and trying to save my great-aunt. Correction—*we* were trying to save her. I wasn't in this alone. My cousins were by my side, both of them. They could have abandoned me but hadn't. Often, when I stood next to them, that song from *Sesame Street* rang in my head—*One of these things is not like the other, one of these things just doesn't belong.* But at that moment I'd never felt more like a family and I might have hugged them if I hadn't been so freaked out.

The Lincoln Memorial towered behind us. I could feel the statue's presence, as if the huge, rugged face was watching over us, guarding our efforts. The Camels stood across the road at the end of the Reflecting Pool. They quickly spotted us. Mr. Camel held tight to Juniper's arm. I wondered why she didn't simply scream for help. Security guards were everywhere. Maybe Mr. Camel had a gun.

"Here we go," Tyler said as Mrs. Camel began to walk toward us.

"I'm having second thoughts," Ethan said, his voice cracking. "Maybe we should—"

"It's too late," I told him, my legs suddenly feeling boneless. I hid the box behind my back.

While Juniper and Mr. Camel watched, Mrs. Camel hurried to the base of the stairway. She wore jeans and a billowy white shirt. Her eyes were accented by thick black liner. Bright red lipstick made it look as if she'd had blood for breakfast. She looked nothing like the old lady she'd pretended to be at the fruit stand. She walked up one step, then another and another until she was only two steps beneath us.

I struggled to find my voice. "How . . . how did you know where to find us?"

"Your aunt wisely decided that your life, Jacqueline Malone, was worth more than the box you hold behind your back. She told us that the Lincoln Memorial was the right spot." She flared her nostrils. I understood why my great-aunt wasn't making a scene—she was worried the Camels still might hurt me. "You haven't opened it, have you? You're not trying to give me an empty box, are you?"

"Kidnapping is against the law," I said, mustering every bit of courage I could find. "And I think the police would be very interested to know all

243

about you and your fake passports."

She flinched, then ran a hand over her short black hair. "You threaten me?"

"Yes," I said.

"Give. Me. The. Box." She sounded as cold as the metal itself. And the look in her eyes was fierce and hungry. She perched on the tips of her toes, ready to pounce like a jaguar and devour me whole.

"Not until you release my great-aunt," I said, trying to hide the quaver in my voice.

She took another step, her fingers wiggling. "Give me the box, now!"

"Everything all right over here, folks?" A security guard moseyed toward us, his blue polyester pants too tight around his bulging thighs.

Mrs. Camel relaxed her hands. "Yes, certainly everything is fine. Just fine. Thank you very much." She smiled sweetly at the guard. After he'd walked away, she narrowed her eyes at me. "Let me make this perfectly clear, in case you are thinking about double-crossing me. If I release your great-aunt, and you decide to keep the box, I will follow you home to Chatham. I will become *your* worst nightmare. Do you understand?"

There was no doubt in my mind that she was

fully capable of becoming my worst nightmare. I was about to say, "yes, I understand" when Tyler pushed me aside, then stepped in front of me.

"Who do you think you are, threatening a twelve-year-old girl?" he asked, his temper flaring. "Because if you're threatening Jax, then you're threatening my family and I wouldn't do that if I were you. My best friend is Walker Ranson and his father is the Chatham chief of police. So intimidation isn't going to work with us. We made a deal. You release Juniper and you can have the stupid box."

Mr. Camel and Juniper waited, out of earshot.

Ethan stopped pinching his nose and he and I exchanged a look of surprise. For the first time ever, I was seeing Tyler in a different light. The gaming geek was acting like a hero from one of his virtual worlds. Suddenly he didn't look so sloppy with his stained T-shirt and uncombed hair. He stood, his shoulders wide, towering over the sinister Mrs. Camel, defending me.

"Oh, and one more thing. I want five hundred dollars, cash, for my broken window. I know you have the money." He held out his hand. Mrs. Camel's face got so tight I thought she might have a stroke. She pulled some bills from her pocket and handed them to Tyler. Tyler counted the bills, then smirked. "Okay then. Objective complete. It's hot, I'm hungry. Let's do this thing."

Anger flashed in Mrs. Camel's eyes, but she didn't argue. She turned and waved at her husband. He let go of Juniper's arm. Juniper stumbled away, unsteady on her feet. "Why is she walking like that?" I asked. "What have you done to her?"

"She's walking like that because she's old," Mrs. Camel hissed. Then she reached out again, her fingers twitching with anticipation. "The box."

I handed it to her.

She inhaled sharply as she gripped the metal edges. Then her eyes narrowed. "You opened it."

"Yes, of course I opened it," I said, as innocently as I could. "It was my birthday present. There was a Starbucks card inside."

Mrs. Camel's expression was pure hatred. No one had ever looked at me like that before and it made my stomach clench. "This isn't over," she said between clenched teeth.

"Oh, it's over," Tyler said. Then he strode down the stairs and went to help our great-aunt, who was staggering through the crowd. Ethan stayed by my side. I could hear his anxious breathing.

Mrs. Camel's gaze burned into mine. "You know how I'm feeling, don't you? You want to protect it. You want to possess it."

I swallowed hard. *Yes*, I thought. *Yes, I know how you feel*. How could I have something in common with this horrid woman?

"You will regret this. Pandora will hear my plea and I will have what is mine." Then she hurried down the steps. She said nothing to Juniper as they passed each other. When she reached Mr. Camel, they both walked swiftly along the Reflecting Pool until they disappeared into the crowd.

24
ETHAN

FACT: *Forget it. There was no time to think about facts.*

I dabbed my nose. The bleeding had stopped. Good riddance metal box. Good riddance Camels. Now it was time for an explanation.

Our Great-Aunt Juniper stood in the middle of the walkway that led to the monument, people streaming past in both directions. She'd taken hold of Tyler's arm for balance. A few days ago we hadn't known anything about her, yet there she was, the cause of all this mess. She motioned wildly at us. "Come on," Jax said, running down the steps.

She looked so much older than in the photos. Her skin was wrinkled and covered in old-age splotches. Her shirt was untucked, her braids were coming undone. Dark circles hung beneath her eyes and a fresh bruise covered her right cheek. There was also a bandage on her right temple. I don't know what I'd expected, maybe a hug for her niece and nephews who'd basically saved her life, but instead she grabbed Jax's shoulders and said, "For the love of God, please tell me you figured it out. Please tell me you have the jar."

"Yes, we have it," Jax assured her, tilting her head toward the backpack.

"Good." She let go of Jax. Her eyes were watery and slightly cloudy. "Did they hurt you? They told me they were going to hurt you. I never intended to put you in harm's way. I . . ." Her eyes brimmed over, tears spilling onto her cheeks. "I'm so very sorry."

"I'm fine," Jax said. "Please don't cry. We're all fine."

"Yeah, we're fine," Tyler confirmed. "But you look like someone beat you up."

Had Mr. Camel used "stronger methods"? How could a man hit an old lady? If he was capable of that kind of brutality, what could he do to Jax? To us?

I handed Juniper a clean tissue. She wiped her

face, wincing when she touched the bruise. I was going to ask her about the blood on the kitchen floor but she wobbled, as if about to faint. Tyler took her arm again. "I'm feeling a bit . . . confused," she said.

"Do you want to sit down?" I asked.

"There's no time," she said. "Give me the jar and I'll be on my way."

"You can't leave. You have to tell us everything." Jax started squirming as a bunch of questions shot out. "Where did you get it? And how come you sent it to me? Why does my mom hate you? And where have you been all these years? Why do the Camels pray to Pandora? And—"

"Yes, of course, I owe you an explanation." She wobbled again. "But I don't want to put you in any more danger."

Tyler raised an eyebrow. "Excuse me, but do you have any idea what we've been through? My car window was bashed in. Jax broke into a motel room. My friend Walker is totally perturbed because we're supposed to be working on level six of Cyclopsville. And Ethan's had about a million nosebleeds because this whole thing has turned him into a basket case. You *owe* us an explanation."

"Uh . . . that's kind of insulting. I'm not a basket

case," I mumbled. "I'm the one who got the box out of the safe, remember?" Give Caution Boy some credit when he deserved it.

Juniper turned her wrinkled face up at me. "You get nosebleeds?" I nodded. "I'm sorry to hear that. I'm afraid you've inherited them from me. Overly sensitive genes."

Inherited? Genes? I almost smiled at those words. I'd always been told that my nosebleeds were psychological. That I was the only one in the family to suffer from them. That if I could just be more confident and less shy, I wouldn't get them.

"Hello?" Jax said. "Can you please tell us about the jar?"

"Yes, of course. But not here. Martha and George won't leave the country without the jar. They will forge a new plan and then come after it."

"Why?" I asked. "Why do they want it so badly?"

Juniper looked very seriously at Jax. "Even if Martha wanted to forget the jar, she wouldn't be able to. It got into her head. You know what I mean, don't you?" Jax nodded. "Only females can sense it."

What was she talking about? Only females?

"And George Camel will use force if necessary. He does whatever his wife tells him to do, just to make her happy." Juniper touched one of the backpack's straps. "Please carry it carefully, as if you were carrying a nuclear weapon."

"A nuclear weapon?" I said, my voice cracking. Two passing tourists turned and looked quizzically at me.

"Lower your voice," Juniper warned.

"Sorry," I said. Wait a minute, why was I apologizing? She'd sent a weapon in the mail and we'd been carrying it around. "It's not really nuclear, is it?"

"No, of course not. But I'm afraid it can be used to hurt other people." She pressed a trembling finger to her temple.

Powers beyond belief. That's what Mrs. Camel had said.

The security guards stood outside the memorial entrance, watching tourists come and go. They weren't paying any attention to us—three kids and an old lady. They had no idea that our backpack contained something dangerous. Backpacks were suspicious items these days. If Tyler set it on the ground and walked away, a SWAT team would be called in. The jar would be confiscated. Maybe that would be an end to all of this.

"Give her the jar," I told Jax between clenched

teeth. "Give her the jar and let's go home."

"No," Jax said. "We've come this far. I want answers."

"Agreed," Tyler said. "The quest is not complete until we get the truth."

I like truth. Facts are true. Science is true. But at that moment, every cell in my body screamed, *walk away*. *Go home*. The truth doesn't need to be known. The truth doesn't always set you free.

"I'll explain as soon as we're in a safe location," Juniper said. Then she began to cross the manicured lawn. Tyler and Jax followed like eager puppies. I reached into my shorts and pulled out a five-dollar bill, all that was left after buying the bag of apples and the chips and doughnuts. Five dollars wouldn't get me back to Chatham. Crud!

Who was I kidding? I couldn't leave. Juniper was no longer a name—she was a person who'd been bruised and battered. She shared my overly sensitive genes. And Tyler might have been a genius, but he didn't always have the best grip on reality. And Jax, who craved adventure, had been acting like someone under a hypnotic spell.

Call me a partner or call me a sidekick, either way, they all needed me.

25
JAX

Hello? I needed answers. Because I felt like I was going to lose it!

Juniper didn't walk very fast. Her steps were unsteady so I took her arm. We might have gone back to our room at the Madison Hotel but she led us in the opposite direction. She said she wanted to stay out in the open, in a public place. "George Camel has a gun. He won't use it if there are witnesses."

"A gun?" Ethan said with a gasp.

"The Camels will do whatever necessary to get the jar." She checked over her shoulder. "All they need is one of us."

She was right. If they threatened to hurt Ethan or Tyler, I'd hand over the clay jar. If they threatened to hurt the great-aunt I barely knew, I'd hand it over. We cared about each other and that made us vulnerable. And yet . . .

Part of me still wanted to keep the jar. A terrible thought gripped my mind—if the jar possessed me, would I risk the people I love? I never wanted to learn the answer to that question.

Even though the jar was tucked into the backpack and hanging from Tyler's shoulders, I could feel its voiceless presence, calling to me in some kind of magical way. So I moved to the other side of Juniper, keeping her between me and Tyler like a human shield. It worked and the feeling lessened, but did not fully go away.

A sign said we were in West Potomac Park. Lots of people strolled through the park, enjoying the sunny day. Juniper started feeling dizzy, so she agreed to rest for a moment. We stopped at a bench along the water. A little boy crouched next to a box of fishing tackle while his father cast a line. In the distance, the Washington Monument pointed at the clear blue sky like an index finger. There was no sign of the Camels.

Tyler had grabbed some sodas from an ice-cream vendor along the way. He popped them open and passed them around. Juniper took a long drink, then unwound her red bandana and dabbed sweat from her forehead. Ethan and Tyler settled at her feet while I sat on the bench next to her. I caught a glimpse of my mom in Juniper's face. They shared the same profile, the same intense expression. She had Ethan's overly sensitive genes but did she share anything with me? I found none of my features in her face. I still looked like the one that didn't match.

"So?" Tyler asked. He removed the backpack and set it on his lap. "Spill it. Tell us."

"She's trying to catch her breath," I said, though I was just as anxious to get some answers. I clutched the edge of the bench, trying my best to ignore the tugging sensation that had returned. I wanted to open the backpack and hold it. But I didn't want to wrestle with those dark thoughts again.

Tyler tapped his feet impatiently. "How come the Camels wrote *Pandora* on their motel-room wall? How come they lit a bunch of candles, like a shrine?"

"How very interesting." Juniper taped a finger on her chin. "They must have been trying to contact her, hoping she would guide them on their quest."

"Contact her?" Ethan nearly choked on his soda. "Uh . . . how can you contact a character from an ancient myth?"

She looked calmly at Ethan. "Do you ever pray?" she asked him. "Do you ever ask God to help you with something?"

Ethan shrugged. "Yeah, I guess. Sometimes."

"Well, that is exactly what the Camels were doing, praying to Pandora to help them."

"But . . ." Ethan wiped soda specks from his chin. "She's not real."

"Says who?" Juniper raised a single eyebrow. "She was as real to the ancient Greeks as your god is to you."

"Did the old jar belong to Pandora?" Tyler asked matter-of-factly. "Is this thing the real Pandora's box? 'Cause that would be totally awesome." Juniper smiled mischievously. Hello? Why was she smiling?

"Uh . . . wait a minute," Ethan said. "It's not a box, it's a jar. So it can't be."

"You are correct," she said. "It is not Pandora's box. But Pandora is the reason it exists." She closed her eyes and pressed her fingers against her temple, over the wound.

"I don't understand." My whole body felt fidgety. I hate it when someone takes too long to tell a story. *Just help me understand*, I wanted to shout. But Juniper was old. She'd been hurt. "Please," I said gently. "Please tell us."

"I shall do my best to explain." She opened her eyes and took another long drink of soda. Then she looked at each of us, and as she spoke, the story took form in front of my eyes, like a movie. And the characters looked oddly familiar.

Beautiful Pandora, the first woman on earth, was given a box by Zeus. She was forbidden to open it but she did, and a cloud of evil swirled from the box and spread throughout the world. Afraid, she closed the box and hid it in her house, vowing to never open it again. But the world remained a dark, horrible place.

I could see my mother, holding the box, trying to stuff it into the trunk of her car.

Time passed. Pandora married a man named Epimetheus. They had a daughter named Pyrrha.

Pyrrha looks exactly like me. But my father has no face. He's just a shadowy figure, standing next to my mom.

One day, Pyrrha found the box and opened it. She discovered that something was trapped at the bottom of the box—Hope. So she released Hope into the world and everything changed. People could now cope with the evil that surrounded them. The world was a better place.

Pandora was overjoyed and so proud of her daughter that she begged Zeus to give her daughter a reward. Zeus gave Pyrrha three jars. One contained Faith, one contained Love, and one contained another dose of Hope. Pyrrha could release these whenever she needed them.

I could see myself holding the old jar.

But Epimetheus, the father of Pyrrha, became jealous. He hated that the gods paid so much attention to his wife and daughter, but never to him. So he stole the three jars and tried to keep them for himself.

His act had serious consequences. The

*jars were designed for one single purpose—to
hold Faith, Love, and Hope for Pyrrha. Only
for Pyrrha. No one else. So when Epimetheus
opened the jars, the contents were destroyed.
The jars were left empty.*

As our great-aunt finished her story, Tyler sat
speechless, mesmerized, as did I. "So are you saying that we have one of the jars?" Ethan asked,
pointing to the backpack. Juniper nodded. "But
you said it was dangerous. How can an empty
jar be dangerous?" He sat with his arms folded, a
scowl of disbelief frozen on his face.

"Well . . . let me try to put this in scientific terms."
She tapped the side of her soda can. "The law of
magnetism is a good analogy. A long time ago magnetism was considered magical. It was believed that
magnets were drawn together by a strange invisible
force. We now know that the force is not created by
magic but by . . ." She smiled at Ethan.

"Electric currents," he said, "caused by moving
electrons."

"So what we once thought of as magic, we now
understand. The law of attraction that pulls the two
magnets together is the same law working in this

situation. The jar that currently rests in your back-pack was designed to hold Hope. It is attracted to hope, much the same way one magnet is attracted to the other."

"Whoa," Tyler said, blinking rapidly. "I get it. If you open the jar, it will seek hope. It's a psycho-logical weapon."

"Yes, exactly." Juniper pushed her long braids behind her shoulders. "Pyrrha's jar seeks hope and when hope is found, the jar takes it. It sucks hope from anyone in the vicinity, leaving its victims in a nearly comatose state." She pushed up her sleeve and scratched at a cut on her forearm.

A nearly comatose state? Suddenly, I began to understand. "Is that what happened to the people in that newspaper article? It said they were work-ing on a Greek island and they all collapsed from a mysterious illness—all but one person."

"How do you know about that?" she asked.

"We went into your house," Tyler explained. "The door was open. The place had been ransacked."

"Martha and George broke in while I was taking a walk. When I confronted them, Martha knocked me in the head and I don't remember much after that. I woke up in a strange place." She continued to scratch the cut on her arm. "We were working together on the island of Kassos. I'm the one who excavated Pyrrha's jar. I didn't know what it was so I opened it. And hope was sucked from everyone at the site, including George and Martha."

"How come you weren't affected?" I asked.

"The only thing I can figure is that whoever holds the jar is immune. The jar needs a protector. The protector does not suffer." She looked at me. "The jar was originally made for a girl, for Pyrrha, but Pyrrha is long gone. So the jar continues to seek a female to protect it. Females appear to be the only ones who can feel it calling. Can you feel it right now, Jax?"

"Yes," I said. Pulling at me. *Hold me. Keep me safe.* I fought the sensation and jumped to my feet as I realized what was at stake. "Why would you send a hope-sucking jar to me? Holy cow! What if I'd opened it? My mom, my cousins, they could have been hurt."

"If they'd been standing near you when you opened the jar, then they would have felt god-awful and they would have looked like zombies, but the effects aren't permanent. Everyone at the site eventually recovered." She ran a finger along her forearm, staring intently at the wound. "But they only recovered because I closed the jar. If it had been left open, I dread to think what would have happened."

My stomach clenched and a wave of panic rolled over me. My mind filled with an image of my mom, lying on the ground, curled in the fetal position. If I'd opened the jar . . . "Hello?" I couldn't believe what I was hearing. "You sent it to me? To me? What if I'd left it open? I could have created some sort of—"

"Zombie apocalypse," Tyler said, practically shouting with excitement. The man who was fishing turned and looked at him. "Totally cool! I've been waiting for the zombie apocalypse."

Tyler wasn't taking this seriously. Ethan said nothing. He just sat there with a giant scowl on his face, disbelieving the entire thing. Juniper looked sorrowfully into my eyes. "I'm sorry, Jax. I didn't plan to send it to you, but I was desperate. Martha Camel figured it out. She knew such a jar could bring great power and wealth. People without hope are easy to control. So she and her husband pursued me. I paid a huge price to have my identity erased and I moved from city to city, trying to keep a low profile. My whole life became dedicated to two things—trying to keep away from the Camels, and trying to destroy the jar. I'd been living in New Hope for only a few weeks when they found me. There was no doubt in my mind that they'd break into the house and do whatever they needed to do to get their hands on the jar. So I panicked. I put it into the puzzle box and mailed it to you. I wasn't thinking very clearly, I'm afraid. The jar makes your thoughts a bit clouded."

Yes, it did. How could I judge her? If the jar continued to work its magic on me, what might I do to keep it safe? How many lives might I risk?

"My desire was to protect it, not to endanger you." Her eyes welled with tears again. "I never meant to hurt you or your family." She wiped her face with the bandana, then slowly rose to her feet. "I shall take Pyrrha's jar and be on my way. There is no need to endanger you any further."

With a burst, Ethan darted to his feet. "Uh . . . guys, we have a problem." We all turned.

The Camels were heading our way.

26
ETHAN

FACT: *There are over 24 million people in the world who have some form of dementia. I was beginning to think our great-aunt was one of those people.*

In order for me to believe any part of her crazy story, I'd have to switch brains with Tyler. Only then could I accept a reality in which a pantheon of Greek gods once ruled the world. Give me a break. A jar that craves hope and sucks it out of people?

And yet I couldn't ignore another fact—so much of her story made sense, in a weird and very unscientific way.

"How'd they find us?" Jax whispered. The Camels were standing way across the park, huddling over something Mr. Camel was holding. They hadn't spotted us. Yet.

"Follow me," Tyler said. He slung the backpack over his shoulder, then dashed toward a bike-rental stand. Jax and I held on to Juniper, trying to move her as quickly as possible. Old people have brittle bones, at least that's what I've read, so I tried not to squeeze too hard. As we stumbled after Tyler, I kept glancing over my shoulder. The Camels were focused on some sort of device. Was it a phone? We reached the stand and hid behind it, out of view of the Camels. But it didn't make me feel much better that the only thing separating us from Mr. Camel's gun was a thin wall of plywood. Tyler peered around the corner. "I see them. I think they've got a GPS unit."

Juniper groaned. "I was worried they might." She touched the wound on her forearm. "It would appear that when they knocked me out, they inserted a tracking device in my arm. I won't be able to evade them until the device is removed."

Jax gulped. "Removed?"

"Do you have a knife?"

I reached into my pocket. "I've got one. A Swiss

266

army knife." But it wasn't there. Had I left it in the motel room, along with my baseball cap? "I don't have it."

"I do," Jax said. She unzipped a side pocket on the backpack and took out the knife. She didn't explain why she'd taken my knife, but I guessed it had something to do with the weird way she'd been acting.

The bike-rental guy paid no attention to us. He was busy with customers. A couple of teenagers who couldn't stop kissing were renting a tandem bike. And a family with a baby was checking out a tow-along contraption that looked like a tent on wheels.

Juniper rolled up her right sleeve. "The wound hasn't scabbed yet. It should be easy to cut out the transmitter." She took the knife and opened it to the sharpest blade.

"Uh . . . wait. The knife's not sterile," I told her. "You could get an infection."

"An infection is the least of my worries," she said. "I can't take the jar to a safe place if the Camels can track me." Her hand trembled as she pushed the blade against her skin.

"Ugh," Jax said, turning away. I knew what she was thinking. It wasn't the thought of piercing the skin, it was the thought of the blood that would leak out.

Juniper sighed. "I . . . I can't do it. I'm right-handed."

"I'll do it," I said. No problem. I'd cut a frog open in biology class. I'd gutted a fish. I could slice open my great-aunt's arm. Why not? Nothing else about this day had been normal.

"No." Jax grabbed the knife. "I want to do this."

Even Tyler was surprised. "You *want* to do it? But you hate blood."

She held the knife tightly. "You guys have done everything—the driving, the directions, you rescued the box from the safe, you stood up to Mrs. Camel. I need to do something. This is important." She gritted her teeth. We closed in around Juniper, hiding her from passersby who might wonder what was going on. As she shut her eyes and gripped my arm for support, Jax pierced the little cut with the tip of the blade. Then, using the knife's tweezers, she pulled out a tiny plastic object, thin and square. It came out easily and there wasn't much blood. "I did it," she said, nearly breathless. She looked at me, smiling with pride. "Did you see that?"

"Yes," I said. "That was amazing." She'd faced

one of her biggest fears. I would have hugged her if there hadn't been a deranged gun-toting couple looking for us.

Juniper dabbed the wound with her bandana. "Thank you," she said. "Now drop that in the dirt and let's get out of here before they find us."

Jax dropped the transmitter. Tyler peered around the corner again. "Crud! They're coming this way!"

We hadn't been fast enough. Mrs. Camel clenched her fists as she powered toward us. Mr. Camel followed, fiddling in his pocket for, I'm guessing, his gun. We had to get out of there! The rental guy was busy. I didn't have much money, but there was nothing else to do. I pulled the five dollars from my pocket and slapped it onto the counter. Then I grabbed a tandem bike. It wasn't stealing, exactly. "Let's go," I said. Jax beamed at me. As usual, I could practically read her mind—borrowing the bikes was a very Jax thing to do.

Juniper climbed onto the second seat and I began to pedal as fast as I could. Tyler and Jax grabbed another bike and we were off. "Hang on," I told Juniper as I veered around a baby stroller. The mom shot me an angry look. I'd never ridden tandem before, so turning was tricky. As we hit a speed bump, Juniper moaned. "Sorry," I said. A flock of pigeons and geese were gathered up ahead, eating bread crumbs that some kids were sprinkling. "Watch out!" The kids jumped out of the way. The birds squawked, and flew to safety. My heart pounded in my ears.

"Crud! The Camels are on a bike," Jax said as she and Tyler rode up next to me. "We should split up. That will confuse them."

"No! The jar must stay with me," Juniper insisted. "Find a crowd. Then I can slip away and you children can go back home and forget any of this ever happened."

Only if I got Alzheimer's would I be able to forget this day. *Only* then.

"There's a crowd," Tyler said, pointing. A tour bus had pulled up to the curb. The door hissed open and a bunch of people started unloading. They all wore orange T-shirts that read, *Number 1 Tours. Because no tourist should feel like a number 2.*

The tour group's destination was the Jefferson Memorial, another gleaming white pantheon-style monument. Like the Lincoln Memorial, there was a colonnade and a wide stairway. This was an open-air structure and the colonnade filtered light into the memorial itself. Of course I knew lots of facts about this place, but no one cared at that moment—not even me.

We ditched the bikes near the tour bus. I held my great-aunt's hand, guiding her until we were in the middle of the group. Some people were taking pictures with their phones; others were complaining about what they'd had for breakfast. Jax and Tyler pushed in next to us. We walked with tiny steps as we squeezed together. I tried not to think about how close everyone was standing. I felt naked without my baseball cap. Tyler stood on tiptoe and looked around. "I don't see them. I think we lost them."

"Everyone inside," the guide announced through a megaphone. "Don't push!"

But everyone did push. Even if we'd wanted to escape at that point, we wouldn't have been able to. Up the stairs we went, like fish caught in a current. Elbows pressed against me, voices rang all around. I started to get dizzy. But then we spilled between the columns and into the memorial chamber. As everyone spread out, I took a deep breath. "You okay?" Jax whispered. "I know you hate crowds."

"Uh . . ." I wiped sweat from my face. "Yeah, I'm okay."

The chamber was round with a high, domed ceiling.

Sunlight streamed through the front colonnade and through the four open portals that were placed around the chamber. Curved wall segments stood between these portals, covered with inscriptions from Jefferson's most famous documents, like the Declaration of Independence. And smack-dab in the center, standing on a podium, was a bronze nineteen-foot-tall statue of our third president. His hair was pulled back in a ponytail and a cloak hung all the way to his feet. The statue was roped off, probably to keep little kids from climbing all over it.

"You have exactly ten minutes to explore the monument on your own," the tour guide said, his voice echoing throughout the chamber. "Then I will give a short presentation on the bus as we head to our next destination." He walked out the front portal and down the stairs. The Number 1 tourists continued to spread out, talking among themselves and snapping photos.

"Now's the time," Juniper said. She'd tied her bandana around her arm, to keep the wound from bleeding. "Give me the backpack and I'll slip out of here. I must get the jar to a safe place." She grabbed one of the straps.

"I don't think you should do this alone," Jax said.

I was about to tell Jax that it would be best if Juniper took the jar. Because we were just three kids from Chatham, New Jersey, and what did we know about archaeological intrigue? Our parents were expecting us to be home that night, safe in our beds, not running from monument to monument, trying to avoid being shot by Mr. Camel or kidnapped by Mrs. Camel. But that's when Tyler said, "They found us."

The Camels stopped in their tracks at the front open portal, watching us. Mr. Camel's hand was still in his pocket. Mrs. Camel glared like a lioness who had spotted her prey. A single security guard wandered the perimeter, more interested in his phone than in his job.

"Would someone explain to me why we don't simply call the police?" Tyler asked. "Because now is probably a real good time."

"We can't let the police get their hands on the jar," Jax said.

"Exactly," Juniper said. "The fewer people who know about its powers, the better."

I didn't argue. The transmitter had been real. The kidnapping and thievery had been real. Whether or not the jar had actually belonged to Pyrrha, those Camels were serious about getting it. They were professional criminals. Calling the police might drive them over the edge and they might decide to attack. "So what do we do?"

"We need a distraction," Juniper said as we huddled at the base of Jefferson's statue. "Something that might stall them and give me a head start. At least enough time to get to a cab."

"I could start crying," Jax said. "I could pretend I broke my ankle or something. That would cause a scene."

"That would bring attention to you but it wouldn't keep the Camels from following me," Juniper said.

"I've got an idea," Tyler said. "In Cyclopsville, one of the ways to defeat the king is to trample him with a stampede of zombies. We could do the same thing here. Ethan could act as a tour guide and try to get everyone's attention. Then he could lead the group over to the Camels and we could trip them up while Juniper makes her escape."

That wasn't such a bad idea, except that it would mean talking to more people than I'd ever talked to, at least triple the size of the Lincoln Memorial group. We all looked at our great-aunt. Her breath was shallow. Perspiration glistened on the bridge of her nose. It had been a fast walk up those stairs. She wobbled, then leaned against Jax.

"I don't mean to be rude or anything," Jax said, "but I don't think you can get away quick enough. You're tired and you've been hurt. We could cause the biggest distraction in the world but you still wouldn't be able to outrun the Camels."

The Camels hadn't moved, their gazes burning into us like acid. The security guard waddled past, texting something and snickering to himself.

"What if we all split up?" Tyler said. "Went in opposite directions. They wouldn't know who to follow."

"Martha would know. She can sense the jar," Juniper said.

I frowned. While "sensing" a jar sounded ridiculous, I couldn't ignore the fact that Mrs. Camel was staring at the backpack, her fingers twitching.

"Then there's only one thing to do," Jax said. "We have to make it so the Camels can't follow any of us. So they can't even move."

"How are we going to do that?" I wondered. But as soon as I asked that question, I knew what she was thinking.

Jax grabbed the backpack. "We have to open the jar."

"No!" Juniper cried.

"Listen to me." Jax lowered her voice so only we could hear. She unrolled her plan like a seasoned general leading the troops. "The effects are only temporary. You said so, right?" Juniper nodded. "So I'll take the jar out of the backpack. Ethan and Tyler will cause some sort of commotion and lead the tourists out of here and back to the bus. If you and I hold onto the jar, we'll be safe. I'll open it just long enough for the Camels to turn into zombies. Then I'll close it."

She looked at me. What was I supposed to say? Part of me believed her and part of me thought this whole thing was impossible. But I sure as heck didn't have a better plan. "If we don't deal with the Camels right now, they'll come after us and none of us will ever be safe," I said.

Tyler raised an eyebrow. "Then let's do this thing."

Juniper nodded. "Agreed."

Jax took the jar out of the backpack and removed the bubble wrap. A change came over her immediately. Her eyes flashed and she hugged it to her chest. Mrs. Camel went rigid as she spied the jar.

"Hurry," Juniper told us.

"I know what to do," Tyler said. "FIRE!" he yelled. "FIRE!"

The security guard looked up. People stopped walking but no one panicked. We were in an open stone building with direct escapes all around us. There were no flames, no smoke. The guard slid the phone into his pocket and hurried toward us.

I took a deep breath. Act confident and no one questions you. I cleared my throat, then stepped over the rope and up onto the podium. Thomas Jefferson towered behind me. "Hello everyone," I said, my hands around my mouth. "May I have your attention please?" Only a few people glanced at me. "May I have your attention please?" I hollered.

They looked up from their phones and maps. Mr. Camel narrowed his eyes with suspicion. Mrs. Camel's attention was frozen, as if nothing else existed in the world but the jar. The security guard pointed at me. "Hey, kid, you're not supposed to be behind the ropes."

I took a deep breath. *Confidence.* "Uh . . . hello everyone. Your ten minutes are over. Please make your way back to the bus." No one questioned me. No one asked who I was or why I wasn't wearing an orange shirt. The Number 1 tourists began to move toward the front exit, but not fast enough. "Uh . . . I don't mean to alarm anyone but the bus is leaving!"

Boy, did they move quickly. The place was deserted in a matter of seconds. Except for the guard. He halted a few feet from our backpack, which lay on the floor. "Does that belong to one of you?" he asked.

"She's having trouble fighting the urge," Juniper cried. "Get out," she told Tyler and me.

Jax's arms were trembling, her breathing fast and shallow. She was muttering to herself. "Protect. Protect." She was possessed.

Tyler began to run. I scrambled off the podium. Jax's hand gripped the plug at the top of the jar. There wasn't enough time for me to make my escape. And there was no time for doubt. I leaped over the rope and pressed my fingers against the side of the jar. The surface sizzled my skin. Juniper grabbed the jar around its base. Jax was shaking like a washing machine on its spin cycle. "Tyler!" I yelled. "Hurry! Get outside!"

The security guard started to back away from us. "What's in that jar?" he asked, a worried look spreading over his face.

Tyler dashed toward the exit but Mr. Camel leaped forward and grabbed him around the waist, shoving a gun into his back. "Don't move!" Mr. Camel ordered. Tyler froze, his hands in the air. "Hand over the jar or I'll kill him!"

My stomach went into a knot. Tyler's life was in danger. We'd failed. We'd—

"Give me the jar!" Mrs. Camel pulled a gun from her shirt and rushed toward us.

"Open it!" Tyler cried. "I'll be okay. Do it now! Don't let them win!"

Mrs. Camel got closer and closer. She pointed the gun at Jax. Her index finger pressed the trigger and . . .

Jax yanked on the plug, pulling it free.

WELCOME TO THE
SECRET BOX CAMPAIGN.

You are logged in as Tyler. You are seventeen years old, in excellent health aside from a few hunger pangs. You are unarmed and there are no weapons currently available. Your strength resides in your superior intellect.

Your team consists of an old lady who's been injured, a twelve-year-old girl who is under a spell, and a thirteen-year-old boy who is prone to nosebleeds. The girl carries a secret weapon.

The enemy is logged in as Mr. and Mrs.

Camel. They are middle aged, in excellent
health. They are both armed with handguns.
Their strength lies in their total dedication
to win at whatever cost.

The enemy's objective:

obtain the secret weapon.

Your objective:

get clear of the weapon before its

powers are unleashed.

Your location is the Jefferson Memorial.
Exits are clearly marked.

Start Game.

The exit was directly in front of me. It was a straight
shot. I could sprint it easily. Nothing stood in the way.
The plan was set into motion. Ethan was right behind
me. I pumped my arms and legs. Get out. Get safe.

Mr. Camel flew at me and grabbed me by the shirt.
He was stronger than he looked and he pulled me to
a dead stop. Then something pressed into my back.
"Don't move," he ordered. I raised my hands into the
air as the gun's barrel dug into my skin. "Hand over the
jar or I'll kill him!"

I turned around. Ethan wasn't with me. He was
holding on to the jar. As were Jax and Juniper. I'd failed.

I didn't know what to do.

"Give me the jar!" Mrs. Camel cried, and she pulled out another gun, aiming it at Jax.

Mayday. Team member captured. Tyler requesting immediate assistance:

The three remaining team members are unable to assist.

Disable enemy's weaponry:

Your health bar is lowered. You are outmatched.

Terminate Game:

Not an option.

Restart Mission:

Restart button disabled.

Define new objective: ?

Define new objective: ?

New Objective:

Sacrifice self to save the team.

The Camels were going to win, they were going to shoot us all and take the jar. How could I stop them with a gun to my back? There was only one way. "Open the jar!" I cried. "I'll be okay. Do it now. Don't let them win!"

When Jax pulled the plug, a wailing sound slithered

from the jar and filled the whole room. It was the worst thing I'd ever heard. Tears welled in my eyes. I began to tremble. Every sad thought I'd ever had seared my mind. Mr. Camel dropped his gun but neither of us moved. I wanted to run from that place but I couldn't.

I had no family. No friends. No one liked me. No one loved me. My bedroom was dark. I sat in front of the computer, its screen a gaping black hole of nothingness. I reached into the hole and pulled out my trophies. They turned to dust in my hands. I tried to flee the bedroom but the door led to nothing. I called out. My voice echoed back at me. I was alone in the world.

The air began to swirl, around and around, and into the jar. As it blew past me I could no longer cry. The sadness was as heavy as cement. Pain invaded my veins. Deep, deep pain. The room turned dark.

The pain turned to fear. I was scared. Very scared. All alone.

I sank to the floor.

Objective Complete
Enemy Disabled
Player Disabled
End Game

28
ETHAN

Wednesday

FACT: *I love my brother.*

I'd never told him I loved him, until I was sitting next to his hospital bed. Maybe it doesn't count when you whisper to someone who's in a coma. But that's what I did. The doctors said Tyler's coma was caused by a virus, though they couldn't figure out which one. His vital functions were sound, so that was a good sign. He lay perfectly still, only his chest rising and falling.

Jax and I said nothing to the doctors. What could

we say? That we had a magic jar that sucked hope from anyone standing near it? Besides, what could the doctors do? There's no scientific cure for something caused by a Greek god. And neither of us wanted to end up in the psychiatric ward. So we visited the hospital's chapel, a tiny room with a stained-glass window where people went to pray. "Ask God for help," Jax said as she knelt. "Ask Pandora for help, too. Ask Zeus and all of them for help." And so I did. I bowed my head and prayed to every god I could think of.

The rest of the time we sat in the hospital room with our parents. Mom held on to Tyler's hand. Dad held his other hand. Aunt Lindsay brought in coffee and snacks from the cafeteria, but no one ate a single thing.

I couldn't stop thinking about what I'd seen. Juniper, Jax, and I had held tightly to the jar. After Jax pulled the plug, it was like some sort of special-effects team had been brought into the Jefferson Memorial. An eerie wailing sound slithered out of the jar—it made my skin crawl. Then wind began to blow, swirling around and around the chamber, sweeping across our faces, through our hair, over our bodies. That's when Tyler, Mr. Camel, Mrs. Camel, and the security guard collapsed. The wind swirled faster and then was sucked right into the jar. Jax trembled through the whole thing. I had to grab her hand and force her to plug the jar. Then I shoved it into the backpack and handed it to Juniper. As soon as the jar left her hands, Jax stopped shaking.

We rushed to Tyler's side. He lay on the floor, his eyes wide open, a look of terror on his face, but he didn't blink, didn't talk, didn't move. Juniper checked for a pulse and made sure he was breathing. "It's just like the last time," she said. "He looks dead but he isn't. He'll recover. They'll all recover."

And exactly twenty-four hours after Jax had unplugged the jar, Tyler opened his eyes. "Hey," he mumbled. "What's everyone looking at?"

Until that very moment, I'd never seen my dad cry. Everyone started crying. "Jeez, what's the matter?" Tyler grumbled. Then he asked for some food.

While our parents were talking to the doctor in his office, Jax and I waited for the nurse to leave, then we sat on Tyler's bed. "What happened?" he asked, his voice deep and groggy. Stubble covered most of his jaw. Another couple of days and he'd have a full beard.

Jax started talking as fast as she could. "Ethan

called 911 and told them that you and a couple other people had gotten sick at the Jefferson Memorial. When the ambulances and police arrived, we pretended like we didn't know the Camels. We didn't have to tell the police anything because they found the Camels' fake passports and guns. As soon as they wake up from their comas, they're going to be sent back to England to face charges of forgery and fraud."

Tyler nodded, but his expression was blank. "What about the security guard?"

"He woke up an hour ago," I told him. "He's in a room down the hall."

"What if he tells them what happened?"

"He doesn't remember anything," Jax said. "We listened at the door while the doctors questioned him."

"I don't remember much either. My head feels thick." Tyler didn't sound like himself. His voice was flat, not flavored by the usual sarcasm. With the circles under his eyes and the yellowish tint to his skin, he looked totally wiped out.

"Juniper got away before the police arrived," I told him. "She took the jar but we don't know where she is. Our parents know nothing. They don't even know that we met our great-aunt. We told them we spent the night at the Madison Hotel. When we found out we had the wrong date for the geocaching competition, we decided to go sightseeing. And then you got sick."

"How do you feel?" Jax asked. "What was it like?"

I didn't want to know the answer. I'd seen the results of having hope stripped from the soul. I'd watched my brother's face contort, his eyes go vacant, his body collapse as if his bones had liquefied.

"It felt bad," he said, the words slow and heavy. "Cold. Like my blood had been replaced by Slurpee juice. I wanted . . . I wanted to stop living. I don't ever want to feel that way again."

How could I make him feel better? "Juniper thinks it won't take long for you to recover. The jar was only open for a second."

"A second?" He winced. "But it felt like forever."

"One second," Jax assured him. "That was it."

"You looked like a zombie," I told him, knowing he'd appreciate that description.

One corner of his mouth turned up slightly. "Cool." Then he peeled the lid of a Jell-O container and slurped it down. "Walker's never going to believe this. He's going to freak out."

"You can't tell Walker," Jax said. "You can't tell

anyone. We promised Juniper. If the wrong person hears about the jar—"

"We could be facing a catastrophe," I said. "Think about it. Look what it did to you in one second. Imagine if it was open for a whole minute? In the hands of a maniac, a nation of hopeless zombies would be easy to control. Or if the head of a corporation had the jar, he could convince anyone to do anything just by threatening to open it. He'd have unlimited power."

Tyler nodded. "Yeah. Okay. I'm not so keen on a zombie apocalypse anymore." Then he raised an eyebrow at me. "So, am I hearing right? You actually believe this stuff?"

Jax looked at me, waiting for my answer. In that moment, we were back in New York City, watching the magician do his "magic" tricks on stage. *It's fake*, I'd told her. *There's no such thing as magic.* I'd doubted everything about the jar but now I knew the truth— we all knew the truth. Fact was indeed stranger than fiction.

"Those Greek gods were crazy," I said.

Jax hugged Tyler. I guess there was a first time for everything. "You're a hero, Tyler. You were so brave."

"You guys were brave too." He set the Jell-O aside,

leaned back against the pillows, and closed his eyes.

Fact: Magic exists. If you have the right tools, you can summon it, and when it reveals itself, it is awesomely powerful.

Fact: Bravery can also be summoned, if you have the right tools, like a younger cousin who pushes you to do things you would never have done on your own. When bravery reveals itself, it is also awesomely powerful.

"You know," Tyler said, his eyes still closed, "I might start hanging out with you more often. Even though you're still a couple of dorkoids." Then he started to snore.

I smiled. He was going to be okay.

29
JAX

Two Weeks Later

It was another record hot day in Chatham, New Jersey. I sat on the front stoop, watching stuff happen. Down the street, a couple of kids were learning how to skateboard. At the corner, a car had broken down and a tow-truck driver was hooking up some jumper cables. A dog walker didn't stop to pick up her dog's poop and Mr. Smith, who'd been trimming his hedge, started hollering at her. His crabbiness didn't bother me as much as it used to. Chatham didn't seem as boring, either. I was looking at the world differently. Guess that's what happens after a major life-threatening event. Sitting and doing nothing in particular seemed perfectly okay.

"Hey," Ethan said. He dumped his bike in the grass, then plopped down next to me. "Tyler's working on his game but he wants to get ice cream with us later." He was wearing the same plaid shorts he'd worn during our adventure. He pulled an orange from his pocket and started peeling. "I heard him laugh today. That's the first time he's laughed since it happened."

"That's good. That must mean he's filled with hope again."

"Guess so." The orange squirted, misting us with its tangy scent. When he was done peeling, he handed me half. "Uh . . . heard anything?"

"No," I said. We'd been waiting for Juniper to contact us. I'd been checking the mail every day, but we'd heard nothing. I still had a gazillion questions for her. "Do you think she's safe?"

"I don't know." He sighed. "Even though the Camels are in jail, there was that other man who called Mr. Camel in the motel. He gave me the creeps. What if he's chasing after Juniper? What if he gets the jar?"

It was almost too scary to think about.

"Jax?" My mom walked outside. She set her car keys and her Chatham Diner apron on the top step, then sat next to me. "I need to leave for work but I wanted to talk to you about something." Her brow was furrowed. Crud. What had I done?

"Uh . . . this sounds serious," Ethan said. "You want me to leave?"

"You might as well stay. It's a family matter and you and your brother will find out anyway." She folded her hands in her lap and focused her gaze on my shoes. "I feel bad that I took your birthday present. I shouldn't have done that. This whole thing with Tyler has made me realize . . . well . . . that time is precious and I shouldn't keep secrets from you. You have a right to know about your father."

I took a sharp breath and dropped the orange. I'd waited for this moment my whole life. "Really? You're going to tell me?"

She frowned and looked into my eyes. "It's not such a nice story, Jax. I don't want you to be disappointed."

So he wasn't a rock star or a prince—big deal. I was prepared for the truth. "Tell me," I begged. Ethan leaned closer, pressing against my arm. How many times had he listened to my fantasies about my father? He deserved to hear this too.

"All right." She tucked her hair behind her ears. "I know you snooped around and figured out the birthday package came from your great-aunt, Juniper Vandegrift." We both nodded. "I haven't spoken to Juniper since you were a baby. I cut her out of our lives because I was angry, *extremely* angry with her. She's the person who introduced me to your father." Mom took my hand. "Of course I wouldn't change a thing, because the result of meeting your father is you, Jax, and I can't imagine life without you."

She was going too slow. "Yeah, I know all that," I said. "I love you too. Don't worry about my feelings. Just tell me."

"Your father was born and raised in Mexico."

Mexico? I looked at her pale hand holding my brown hand. "I'm half Mexican?"

"Yes."

"Cool," Ethan said. "Maybe you can get dual citizenship."

"Keep talking," I told her.

"Well, there was a short time when Juniper worked in Washington, DC, for an archaeological society. Your father was getting his college degree and he worked as an intern with Juniper. That's when I met him. And we fell instantly in love. He was . . . very good-looking. He's the reason why you're so beautiful." She pushed a strand of hair from my face. "I moved to DC and we got married without telling anyone. And then I got pregnant and had you. One day, we met your great-aunt in the city and went for a walk at the Lincoln Memorial. Your father took a picture of you and Juniper; then he handed me the camera and I never saw him again. A few weeks later, Juniper told me the truth. He wasn't a student. He'd been hired to do secret work."

"What kind of work?" Ethan asked. I could barely speak at this point. My thoughts were racing.

"Your father is a professional thief. Or *was* a thief, I really don't know if he's even alive at this point. But he wasn't an ordinary thief. He was a genius. He knew how to break codes, how to disable security systems, stuff like that. The archaeological society hired him to retrieve some sort of artifact that had been stolen from them. That's why he was working in DC with your great-aunt. And then he disappeared because someone was looking for him. He had to go into hiding. Juniper knew where he was but she wouldn't tell me. She assured me that he was a good person. But she said she had to protect him because there was so much at stake. I told her to stay away from me and my family. If she'd been honest with me from the beginning, I wouldn't have allowed myself to fall in love with him." Mom's eyes welled with tears. "It was a very difficult time in my life. I was alone with a baby to support. I blamed her."

It started to make sense. The reason I looked different. The reason my mom had been so protective. "That's why you got mad when I took that candy bar," I realized. "You said you didn't want me to become a career criminal."

"Yes." She wiped her eyes with her sleeve. Then her phone buzzed. "Crud, I'm late for work." She pulled me close, squeezing me real tight. "I love you, Jax. I'm sorry I didn't tell you the truth. We can talk more about this later tonight." She grabbed her keys and apron and started down the steps.

"Wait," I said. She turned. "What's his name?"

"His name is Isaac Romero. But Juniper said he had a special code name. The Locksmith." She hurried toward her car.

Ethan dropped his half of the orange and grabbed my arm. "Did you hear that?" His eyes got real wide and his voice cracked. "Did you *hear* that?"

"Hello? I was sitting right here. Of course I heard it." I forced myself to stay very still, to look as if nothing unusual had just happened. I waited until Mom had backed her car out of the driveway and was driving off. Then I jumped to my feet. "My father's the Locksmith!" I cried. "He built the secret box for me. He set it to open at the Lincoln Memorial because that's the last place he saw me."

Ethan smiled back at me.

I didn't have to imagine him. He was real. I ran across the yard and grabbed my bike. "Come on!" I called.

I rode and rode and rode, past the houses I'd seen hundreds of times. Past the churches and gas stations and stores I knew by heart. For the first time in my life I felt like a whole person, like one half of me was no longer just an outline. After a while, Ethan took the lead, his baseball cap guiding the way as we wound around the school and down to the river. I got all sweaty but I didn't care. It felt good to pump my legs.

This was my town.

This was my family.

This was important.

Acknowledgments

Writing this story has been a wonderful adventure and I have the amazing editorial team of Melissa Miller, Claudia Gabel, and Lynn Weingarten to thank. Katherine Tegen Books is a lovely place for a writer to call home. Thank you.